URANIANS

URANIANS

STORIES

THEODORE McCOMBS

ASTRA HOUSE
NEW YORK

For information about permission to reproduce selections from this book,
please contact permissions@astrahouse.com.

This is a work of fiction. Names, characters, places, and incidents are products of the
author's imagination or are used fictitiously. Any resemblance to actual events,
locales, or persons, living or dead, is entirely coincidental.

Astra House
A Division of Astra Publishing House astrahouse.com

Library of Congress Cataloging-in-Publication Data TK
ISBN: 9781662601941

This is an advance reader's edition from uncorrected proofs. If any material from
the book is to be quoted in a review, please check it against the text in the final
bound book. Dates, prices, and manufacturing details are subject to change or
cancellation without notice.

Design by Richard Oriolo
The text is set in Filosofia OT.
The titles are set in Plaza Grotesque.

"If the day is coming as we have suggested—when Love is at last to take its rightful place as the binding and directing force of society (instead of the Cash-nexus), and society is to be transmuted in consequence to a higher form, then undoubtedly the superior types of Uranians—prepared for this service by long experience and devotion, as well as by much suffering—will have an important part to play in the transformation. . . . This may be saying little or nothing in favor of those of this class whose conception of love is only of a poor and frivolous sort; but in the case of those others who see the god in his true light, the fact that they serve him in singleness of heart and so unremittingly raises them at once into the position of the natural leaders of mankind."

—Edward Carpenter, *The Intermediate Sex: A Study of Some Transitional Types of Men and Women*, 1912

CONTENTS

URANIANS

TOWARD A THEORY OF ALTERNATIVE LIFESTYLES

I. A LOAF OF PETER KAZIMIRS

Peter Kazimir looked miserable in sleeveless black shirts. The fitting room's slatted door was draped in unhelpful layers of baggy, drop-arm, and slashed tees and tanks, all black, and the sales clerk kept tossing more cuts and sizes on top of them, but the color flattened him, and fundamentally, he was a gangly, sallow monkey with arms too long for his torso, and the solid loaf of Peter Kazimirs extending forward and back in the facing mirrors, infinitely multiplied, promised he would never be anything else. He banged out of the fitting room and on to the men's apparel floor but stopped short when he saw Francisco wasn't there.

Fran, Fran, he called over the mannequins and shirt racks, reddening. It didn't take much, these days—three weeks after their breakup—for Peter to feel abandoned. In giant ads on the department-store columns, giant, beautiful people leaned forward out of steel-blue voids, their glances heavy and smoky.

Fran, severely: What? I was looking at sockies.

Peter hugged the mess of black clothes to his chest. Nothing fits, he said.

Fran wore a cut-off band shirt and rubbed his arms to warm himself. The mall, like all of Miami, was over-air conditioned. It was a muggy, glaring, boiling summer outside, the kind of weather meant for fleeing; it was a grayer, cooler summer in Berlin, where they were headed in a week for Peter's birthday. Peter was turning twenty-nine and although Fran had left him—they were kaput, split, Fran had moved out all his stuff—still Peter hadn't let Fran out of the trip. The tickets were nonrefundable, and he needed Fran there to help him get into Collider.

Collider, where everyone wore black, was the club where people like Fran went— scruffy, sulky queers looking for heavy synth beats and faceless sex in a corner—but it was so underground and real, and admission so coveted, that straight men held hands in queue and sissied their voices just to have a shot at the door. It was the world capital of hypnalectronica, and though the club cultivated a strict code of silence, through the cracks came whispered stories of veil-lifting, of visions of alternate universes.

The door policy was strict, too: nothing but black, no large groups, don't talk or laugh in line, don't look too clean. No nice shoes, but boots, sneakers, shoes you could dance in for eight hours. Someone had designed an app that would look at you through your phone's camera and tell you if you'd get in, but Peter already had a healthy persecution complex and didn't need his devices turning against him. Fran had gotten into Collider each of the four times he'd visited Berlin and would get Peter in, too—given the proper wardrobe.

Fran had been reluctant about Peter's self-makeover; Francisco K. Bazán, Esq., had his lawyerly misgivings. Just be yourself, he'd said, in his unruly Cuban accent. But for the entire two years and one month of their relationship, Fran had lobbied for Peter to be somebody very different from himself, and it was too late now to switch to platitudes.

They'd met in New York at an LBGT lawyers' meet-and-greet: Peter, the paralegal at a one-name divorce shop, and Fran, the junior associate at a white-shoe Midtown firm. Neither one had bored the other, always a promising sign. Both were pleased to find someone at the event who looked with any interest above the horizon of gay professional ambition. Fran struck Peter as something beautiful and barely contained: his long, aristocratic face was freshly shaved but already shadowing; his black hair was combed flat, but wavy, and his bushy brows unplucked. He had a master's in Philosophy of Science and a Feynman diagram tattooed across his collarbone, visible when he leaned close and loosened his tie. Peter's knees went buttery, Fran led him into a bathroom stall and yanked his pants down, and Peter burst into tears and confessed in breathy shudders how he was sick of one-night stands, and he wanted a boyfriend, for once, a real boyfriend. Fran, mortified and offended, listened gallantly enough. It was a testament to them both that Fran had taken Peter's number and had called him anyway. But for two years and one month, Fran seemed to wait in that stall for the Peter who'd followed him there, convinced there was another, truer man concealed under all his romantic hysteria. Someone who'd go out with Fran to techno parties, to leather bars, to protests and punk shows. And Peter had taken up the humiliating task of explaining he'd given Fran the wrong idea; he really was the conventional— homonormative—cliché. He really did want to shop for bathroom fixtures together and sit on the same side of a restaurant booth. He wanted to see *La Traviata* in box seats, like in *Pretty Woman*, or meet at the top of the Empire State Building, like in *Sleepless in Seattle*, and not because he'd failed to grasp the false consciousness of the heteropatriarchy, but because he'd spent his life being shown and then denied this way of being in love, and now he was a grown-up, and he could get the things he saw on TV. So, they'd tried it Peter's way. Peter saved up for a new suit and they went to a gay bar styled as a private club, with a snobby dress code and potted rubber trees, and bartenders in tight tuxedo shirts and black velvet bowties, and warm lamps reflected in mahogany paneling. The crowd skewed older and elegant. Peter drank gimlets and warbled about the Metropolitan Opera, and Fran wondered if the universe was a hologram, until Peter went to wash his hands, and when he came back, Fran was furiously explaining to a pearl-haired man in a silver double-breasted that he wasn't a hooker. The silver man called Fran coy. And that's what the bar was, they realized: all the well-dressed young men of color hung beside mature white gentlemen like this asshole, and while Fran sometimes passed for white, his accent gave him away. That night, Fran didn't want to be touched. When they did have sex, in the months after, dark emotions humidified the room: jealousies, resentments, a grave dominance from Fran and a cringing sweetness from Peter that shamed them both. Differences clarified. Fran chafed at monogamy and Peter lost color at the idea of cruising. Fran smoked and Peter asked him to quit. But when Fran got a job in Miami, Peter followed him—to risk everything for love, what could be more exciting?—and together they leased a high-ceilinged one-bedroom in Brickell, and Fran left him ten weeks later. At the time there were brush fires raging in the Everglades and the sky was a foggy, nuclear orange, blowing with ash. One afternoon, they'd gone out for Cuban coffee with an old friend of Fran's, J.B., a Haitian butch activist with mild dwarfism, and J.B. and Fran had railed together over a recent profile of gay newlyweds in *New York Magazine*. The men in the photos wore matching, pastel sweater vests and identical cowlick haircuts; they were young, smiling, tidy, their skin white as candles. One posed with an old book on the couch, while behind him his husband gleefully vacuumed. J.B. fumed: This isn't radical, this isn't queer. Fran mimed vomiting. Out on the patio, they squinted into the bruised air and Peter spat ash from his lips. He said, But what if this is what they want? Fran looked at Peter with pain and reproach, the way he did whenever Peter told an embarrassing story about himself. Peter asked, Is it so wrong to want to be normal? Even with J.B. right there, who would never be let into that word, *normal*, Peter had asked, Is it so wrong to want to be normal? And so, as they drove back to Brickell, in the blur of ashfall, Fran apologized to him (in that seething, accusing parody of an apology) for not seeing the truth of their relationship sooner.

As if the truth of their relationship were so inevitable, and not something hidden in the dark palm groves in parks, late at night, where Peter, trembling, now hunted for it alone.

Peter had kept the Brickell apartment, and by day it wasn't a problem. He subbed as a music teacher for several Catholic schools and rehearsed with the local Gay Men's Chorus. But at night, the apartment pushed him out. He drove and cruised the college campus bathrooms or wandered the obscure lawns of Paradise-Bird Park. Asking himself: Is this really so terrible? Had this been so truly impossible, when he was with Fran, for him to even try? Maybe the distance between him and Fran hadn't been unbridgeable after all. In the dark, Peter hardly knew himself: "Peter Kazimir," who's that?

Peter hadn't told Fran about any of his nights in the park but was tempted to, whenever Fran hinted that Collider wasn't Peter's scene. Be yourself—but in Collider there were glimpses of alternate realities, in which Peter might be another man entirely.

Fran needed socks so they bought socks. The department store's PA system hyped a sale on foundations and concealers. Peter lingered over the underwear packages and their photos of chiseled, headless torsos. If I wear these, he joked to Fran, waving the box, will my chest look like this? Peter had a runner's body, a handsome body that bottomed out into gawkishness the longer one looked. In high school, a modeling scout had once approached Peter in a mall but by the end of the conversation had taken back his business card. Fran hated it when Peter told this story.

II. EVERETT'S MANY-WORLDS INTERPRETATION

In quantum mechanics, a particle's position-space wave function maps the probability of the particle being at any given point in space at a given time. When an observer measures where it "really" is, the wave function collapses into one definite location; unobserved, the particle "is" a little bit everywhere. The act of observation is thus destructive, flattening: every particle is an ensemble of self-versions until fixed by someone else's gaze.

This is the majority theory, called the Copenhagen interpretation.

But under the many-worlds interpretation, all locations described by the wavefunction exist at once, happen at once, and persist side-by-side as alternate realities. Observation doesn't collapse the alternatives so much as pair off the observer with the particular value observed, like dance partners waltzing off in one direction, while, in a parallel reality, the observer pairs off with a different partner in another direction. Every moment generates uncountable parallel realities, capturing each quantum possibility. The majority of these realities are indistinguishable, with maybe a single molecule dog-eared this way or that. But if it's true that everything you do and think is nothing more than a traffic of electrons in your brain, then every possible version of you exists somewhere; and in at least one of those realities, somewhere, necessarily, you got everything you ever wanted, and were loved as much as you loved.

This is the promise of Collider's hypnalectric visions: the lure of seeing yourself perfectly satisfied.

III. THAT NIGHT IN THE PARK

And that night in the park, as Peter skulked and trawled, and as the swollen air clung to his skin and mosquitoes whirled in clouds around the harsh path lights, he met with a shock a man he'd known in New York. Neither said anything. Breath was short, adrenaline off the charts, and any friendliness would have punctured the moment. Besides, Peter hated him a little. The guy was mean, dark-haired, and pretty. In New York, he'd mocked Fran's accent and teased Peter for being poor. They slid off their sandals and their toes dug into the clay. Peter, shaking, flipped him round and ran his hands under the man's loose tee, over his belly muscles and ribs—he was so compact, the hips neat, his balls precise, the flesh of his ass chilly but the pucker hot, so that when Peter entered him he thought of hot laundry, his cock in beautiful clothes out of the dryer; he planted his nose against his neck and smelled salt and hot white sand and faded banana lotion, which made him dig in frenziedly, knocking, insisting. His shorts fell off his thighs and down to his ankles in a jangle of keys. Mosquitoes pricked between the hairs of Peter's calves, drinking as he crouched and pushed.

After, they rinsed themselves at a dribbling water fountain. They found a trash bin and hid the condom under fast-food wrappers. They finally greeted each other, rediscovering language in drowsy fragments, catching up: Peter, single, the other on vacation. Peter picked memories like clothes off the floor: You married your guy, aren't you having a baby? Peter had seen photos on social media of them with their surrogate. He didn't ask if these kinds of hook-ups were cooked into the marriage or not. Predawn light glowed between blue palm trunks. The man—Ryan, his name was Ryan—kissed him on the cheek and invited him to dinner.

So, on Saturday, Peter had dinner with the husbands in South Beach and brought Elgin. Elgin ("like the Marbles"), his dating-site date from a week before: a sweet, skinny Sarasota kid who walked a beagle around Miami International Airport for Customs. Peter knew dinner parties made for chancy second dates, but the thought of eating alone with the husbands was too demoralizing. Elgin was cute but painfully quiet, and Peter had to carry the conversation for him. Tell them about the animals, Peter prompted him. Tell them about the suitcase filled with live crabs. Through a balcony door, the ocean panted softly. Peter watched Ryan swish from kitchen to table and thought of his tiny, warm asshole and his face pressed into a tree.

People try to smuggle live animals through Miami, Peter said; he was still trying to tell Elgin's suitcase-full-of-crabs story. Elgin once caught a woman in a duffel coat full of finches.

Finches? Did you say finches, like the birds?

Yeah, Elgin said at last. They can be really valuable.

(Everyone waited for him to say more.)

She drugged them, Peter said, fifteen of them, then rolled them in socks. Cuban finches, the super-colorful ones. Only four survived. Some get crushed, some freeze, some never wake up from the drugs. People go nuts for exotic pets, it's crazy.

The two husbands held hands on top of the table, and in their free hands, held cigarettes and wine glasses. Their union had a tinge of dominance display to it, like this was one more thing they'd beat everyone else at; same-sex marriage was barely a year old in the State of New York and it was still anyone's game. When Peter had first come out, he'd fallen hard for guys like these, with their perfect muscle tone, whitened teeth, and fascist haircuts, who competed in gay volleyball leagues and took poppers to bottom because every cord and tissue in them was strung so tight. For years, Peter had made a ghoulish pass at looking like them. Now, he thought Fran's crooked teeth handsomer. Now, he felt drawn to flaws, moles, crow's-feet, stray hairs growing below the knuckle. That's what Collider looked for at the door, Fran told him: no one too perfect. Someone life has knocked around a bit. Peter thought: Why did I come here? Who am I trying to impress?

He caught Elgin's hand and squeezed it. So, now they were all holding hands.

They opened a second bottle and Peter told them about his Berlin plans and Collider. You remember Fran, right? he said. In New

York, Peter had often deployed Fran in conversations to intimidate his friends.

The philosophy guy? Ryan said. The quantum guy.

Paul, his husband, narrowed his eyes and pouted around his cigarette, apparently doing an impression: I fuckin' hate erryone an errythin'.

Philosophy of Science, Peter said. Ontology of quantum states in a many-worlds model, that sort of stuff. Like, what's the reality of some other you that you meet at Collider?

You guys were made for each other, Ryan said, grimacing.

And Peter thought that might be true, and he hoped it was, but lately he was more alert to the gaps in this making. All those weak spots in the joinings he'd scrambled to reinforce, until the whole structure came down on him. Heroic/pathetic. After Fran moved out, Peter had gone to the library and brooded over copies of the books Fran took with him, the quantum stuff, the paradoxes, books of epistemology, everything-theories, and spooky action at a distance. As if these ideas still entangled them—or maybe only out of a despairing urge to understand, if not Fran, or himself, then at least the universe.

You know you don't actually see parallel realities, Ryan said. It's just a hallucination brought on by the music and the drugs. It's stupid stoner shit.

I saw myself once, Elgin said. In a club here.

Everyone turned, as if surprised to see him there.

My alternate-reality self, I mean, Elgin said. I might have been in front of a mirror. But in the mirror, I had glasses on. I don't wear glasses. That's what a lot of people see, I've heard.

Elgin flattened his hand across his eyes, and said: Glasses, on people not wearing glasses.

I was at a club in Chicago once that was playing hypnalectronica, Ryan continued. Filthy place. I start to hallucinate, and it's just people coming down the stairs towards me. That's it—down, down, into the basement. Random people of all kinds coming in. I'm like, What's the fucking point of this?

But Collider's different, Peter said. The visions are different. They're life-changing. Fran's been there four times.

Did his life change four times, then?

Peter blushed. Privately, he suspected that the last time Fran had gone to Berlin he'd seen a reality where he lived in Miami and was single.

Peter excused himself to use the bathroom. He tried door after door, swatting at the run of dark walls for a light switch. It's through the bedroom, Paul shouted. The apartment belonged to their surrogate's parents and the bedroom walls were crowded with family photos. After he peed, Peter lingered over these; he held up his phone and ran its blue light over grainy wedding-dinner horrors, red-eyed brides and big-haired grooms; over birthdays, anniversary dances, prom night; ordinary rhythms of unremarked lives. Peter pictured the husbands with a bedroom wall like this, the stations of a marriage, and a daughter swinging between them by her skinny arms. Would one watch her while the other slunk off to the park? He asked himself if he'd have sex with a little girl's father. The thought felt gross, not exactly wrong, but gross and intrusive, like—well, it felt like coming drunk to a two-year-old's birthday party and barfing all over the clown. Wouldn't that be a betrayal of the movement? Or would *not* fucking a dad be the betrayal of the movement? He pocketed his phone. He'd violated some norm by staying so long in the bedroom. Yet he didn't move, and in the dark, the ambient light from the street settled yellow jewels into the picture glass.

Could Fran and I have had this? he wondered. If he could have been a little more of who Fran wanted, edgier, weirder, bruised. If he'd tried harder at it, could he have won Fran over to—what, exactly? A church wedding? Mendelssohn on the organ, rice grains in their shoes? No, even the fantasy came out malformed. They'd be one of those crazy couples that dressed their dogs in costumes.

But *could* they have had this?

When he'd first started training his baritone into a tenor, Peter had sung under a dread of parody, worried the natural tenors would think he was mocking them. He'd sounded pinched and shrill—which was how Peter secretly felt all tenors sounded. In anxiety dreams, Peter stood by the piano in master class, everyone sitting too close, and his voice cracked. He clutched his throat, stricken, asking, Is it because I suck cock? Was the recurring pressure of glans and corona on the back of his throat physically damaging his voice, like smoking, or yogurt?

O dolci mani, mansuete e pure . . .

Peter checked his fly and went back into the living room. Elgin-like-the-marbles was on the sofa between the two husbands, sitting hip to hip, hands on each other's thighs. They looked up with sheepish grins.

I'm going for a walk, Peter said irritably.

He walked along the beach holding his shoes, listening to the waves sizzle on the mud. The moon reflected in the silky black strip where the tide withdrew, but the sand was still warm between his toes. Ahead, the posh South Beach hotels were lit up in green projections. A bass pulse drifted through the humid night air. On their date the week before, he and Elgin had snuck inside one of those patio night-clubs, hurrying through the ultraviolet hotel lobby like they belonged. The slick music bored them, and they'd left. Even so, whenever he spotted those green pavilions against the night ocean, Peter couldn't shake the suspicion he was missing out on something magnificent.

How Fran had described Collider: There I'm not a brown queer with a heavy accent in a fucking law firm. I can just party and it's not a fight. Here, I have to fight every day.

Peter stared back up the beach, where behind one of those windows, the husbands were poaching his date. What's the fucking point of this?

Life disappoints, but in here you are perfectly satisfied—every club or bar promises it, and every one of them lies. And yet, he recalled moments from his just-uncloseted early twenties: moments of weird time brought on by one-dollar well drinks, strobing club lights, the reek of vodka, limbs jellied from dancing and walking everywhere; moments when the universe reached him slowly, as if blunted, when the crowd's damp heat and a slurring backbeat fattened the seconds into little rooms he could live inside. A thing close enough to happiness, like a trompe l'oeil ceiling in a church, promising a deferred heaven to look up to, to get into.

Peter laid himself out on the wet sand, and the hot heavy night pressed down on him like a microscope slide.

IV. EXPERIMENTAL TESTING ALL BUT IMPOSSIBLE

Hypnalectronica and its rumored hallucinatory effect have never at-tracted serious attention outside the techno scene itself. Debunkers have written blog articles claiming they tried it and saw only the world as it was; the believers admit there's an element of self-hypnosis to the visions, and so those who come in determined to resist will re-sist, and succeed in experiencing nothing. This makes experimental testing all but impossible.

No reputable neuroscience or physics could accommodate musi-cally induced visions of parallel universes, of course. One study, never published, did attempt to test the effects on white rats, reasoning that animals, like lovers, are incapable of skepticism. The researchers administered the drugs and music to the rats and ran them through glass-topped mazes; but the rats only stared unnervingly up at the experimenters.

V. THE GAME AT FRAN'S PARENTS' HOUSE

The day before their flight to Berlin, Peter and Fran watched the Eu-rocup game at Fran's parents' house in Kendall. Fran's three older brothers came too, with their wives and girlfriends. Señor Bazán, a sinewy old man who'd once taught German literature but now was a professional gardener (and seemed indifferent to the change), wel-comed Peter stiffly, pronouncing his name Russified, "Pyetr." Fran hadn't told his family about the breakup. They'd been too eager to meet the boyfriend they'd heard so much about, the one who made their moody son smile in photos, and Fran was too proud to admit he and Peter hadn't worked out.

The breakup did feel like some unaccountable fuck-up on both their parts, from this vantage, as they took up the act of a happy couple and found it easy. Peter cleaned his plate twice, got tipsy on wine and buzzed on coffee, he cracked up Fran's mother with his plucky, chirping Spanish and sang snippets of Schubert for Sr. Bazán. In short, Peter charmed them, diligently. The focus and caution this demanded of him was nerve-racking. Fran's parents didn't speak English and his brothers' teasing had sharper edges than Peter was used to; they called their mother "Vieja" or "Gorda," which seemed rude, and him "Flamenco," which sounded mildly derisive. Still, Fran was grateful. Anxious, but grateful.

You're doing great, Fran said, leaning over, squeezing Peter's thigh. How do you like them?

I told a joke! I feel I'm missing every other word, Peter whispered. They keep talking to me about Paco. Who's Paco?

Me.

(Peter, stunned, grinning like a lunatic.)

Fran, drolly enduring transparency: So, now you know.

Across the table, Fran's father regarded Peter skeptically. He spoke little, and then only in an opaque Cuban dialect that Fran neglected to translate. As the meal wore on, Peter suspected that Sr. Bazán considered him trivial.

And why not? The family had fled Cuba in the last exodus, the six of them crashing up Marathon Key on a half-sunk raft. Eighteen years ago, thirty thousand rafters tried the Straits of Florida, riding front doors and bathtubs lashed to tire tubes. Thousands had died—in storms, in shark waters. Thousands more were intercepted by the Coast Guard and penned at Guantánamo. What must Florida have meant to them, what parallel world did they imagine, to risk death like that? But Fran, just sixteen, had been outed by a hostile class-mate and denounced to the secret police. For his family, it was as sim-ple and brutal as that. They'd left. The story made Peter flush with shame. He'd done nothing so heroic as escape Communist persecu-tion. He had no flock of brothers ready to leave everything they'd ever known to protect that most vulnerable, inconvenient part of him. Peter understood his awe for this story irritated Fran—as if Fran's life were an exotic drama for others to be moved by—but he couldn't help getting excited and fearful whenever there was any reference to it. Fran carried his family's sacrifice restlessly, conscious of a debt he could never pay down. Fran was alive; he was Americanized; he was a middling successful lawyer who sent his parents money and a white, Catholic boyfriend. What was enough happiness, here? And Peter realized, as he charmed Fran's family—Peter and Fran real-ized it together, locking glances across the back patio, as the sun set over the canal—that Peter was being charming and perfect for Fran's sake, as if to justify to Sr. Bazán that saving his son's life had been worth it. The old man sat forward in his plastic chair, scratching the swaybacked family bulldog behind the ears, looking tired and home-sick and talking impenetrably of untranslated ideas.

VI. THE CHURCH'S STANCE

The Catholic Church would have no stance on hypnalectric visions, these things normally being beneath its attention, but for the enthu-siasm of a failed seminarian who visited Collider and came out claiming he'd seen Heaven itself and his own glorified body. The Mir-acle Commission grudgingly investigated, then rejected his claim, on two grounds. First, Heaven is characterized by an indispensable inaccessibility: generally, to the human senses (*"eye hath not seen,"* etc.) and specifically, to sinners—by its unbridgeable distance from druggy gay babylons like Collider. Second, Heaven is not a "place" at all, not some other location in reality, but a state of relationship. One theologian put it this way: just as those who have died still exist, in some meaningful sense, in the heart-memory of those who loved them, so too the purified souls continue to exist, in an eternal and perfect sense, in the divine memory. Thus Heaven is not another universe to be discovered and broken into, or glimpsed through a strip of spacetime rubbed bald, but God's immediate, living *theoria* of you—His perfect, loving perception.

VII. THE FAR BACK OF THE LINE INTO COLLIDER

In the bleary half-light and chilly air of four a.m., Peter and Fran waited at the far back of the line into Collider. Muffled techno thumped and oontzed from inside the decrepit East Berlin power plant. The city tapered off here: unkempt lots bordered the old plant, thatched with pale grass and fenced in chain link, and the tallest structure was a billboard for a hardware store. Sparrows chirruped in the trees. Instead of going to bed early and waking up at three to come here, as planned, they'd stayed up all night—roving from bar to club, powered by amphetamines and currywurst. Peter's knees ached. His feet felt like bags of blood. They'd hiked through all of Kreutzberg, threading crowds, dancing in and out of gutters choked with orange drifts of cigarette butts, chattering crazily about art and particle physics, eyes on a never-dark horizon bristling with construction cranes. Steel dinosaur necks towered over domes, crenellations, mansards; there were cranes everywhere, Fran said, each time he'd visited Berlin.

One year ago, ten. It was a city of perpetual reconstruction, building and rebuilding itself. The walk by the Spree was wattled in huge over-head networks of blue waterpipes, gray under the lamps—they were pumping the river out of a new Ubahn tunnel.

Is that a necessary consequence of physics, Fran was saying, electrons *had* to be that way, not heavier, not lighter, because strings, Planck mass, it's like—(Fran had snorted speed in the cab and for twenty minutes, he'd been trying to explain string theory)—or do they just *happen* to have those masses and spins and values they do, like my eyes happen to be brown and yours happen to be blue? *Could* they be different?

Peter looked ahead—everyone knew not to talk excitedly in line, it made you look like an asshole.

On the flight from Miami, Fran had upgraded and left him in coach. They'd napped in their chilly hotel beds, clam-skinned and moldy from travel, then showered together without touching.

My eyes are more hazel, Peter said.

Goths, punks, and art fags, the beautiful and the almost repulsive, thickset and skinny, young and never-young, and everyone dreary in black. Black boots, black rolled trousers, sissified gymwear, coach shorts, black tube socks, studded harnesses. Peter surveyed the oth-ers in queue and thought, I can pass. Peter slouched, put on his grim-mest face. I can do this. The glassy morning light, the combination of intense jet lag and inverted hours, and the dry and bony hectic-ness of the drugs, all of it convinced him he'd get away with any-thing. All constraints were suspended. There were good odds he and Fran would wind up having sex inside, in front of some of these same people. I can do that, Peter thought.

Taxis idled at the curb, ready to shuttle back those who'd come only to be dismissed at the door. By a coffee kiosk, a huddle of young Americans in tight black tees traded consolations, snickering over the ugly doorman and listing the exclusive nightclubs they got into in New York. Techno sucks anyway, one insisted, it's just the worst. The morning was warm but their water-balloon biceps shivered under their hands. Peter didn't hide his satisfaction at seeing them disappointed.

Peter? Fran said, shaking his arm. I'm talking about a different universe with totally different physics. And in that universe, let's say electrons are a little heavier, and it's enough to keep atoms from forming. The stars, the planets, all that never forms; it's just soup. So—what if things are this way and not that way not by necessity, not by *law*, but because it's the physics that makes us possible? That makes any life at all possible? Peter, isn't that beautiful? Our universe is how it is because it's the one *we* can be in. Out of all the theoretical universes, only the one that produces *us* to see and measure it is real. All the others, the soup universes, if they exist, their existence is the same as nonexistence because it's unexperienced.

They'd reached the part of the line enclosed in aluminum cattle rails. An elderly man in a threadbare jacket stooped and gathered bottles left beside the pales into his bag. Peter looked down and realized Fran had not let go of his arm.

Under the feeble dawn, Collider loomed against the dirt fields. Peter asked, Have you ever seen me in there?

Fran bladed his hands into his jean pockets. He dragged on his cigarette and squinted thoughtfully.

The people in front of them dropped away. Fran stepped forward and Peter sidled behind him, like they'd planned. The doorman was a bald, pale, muscular man in a black tee, his scalp white and stippled like a frozen chicken. His eyes, alert and cold. The universe that measures itself. To the left of the doorman, up three stone stairs, an old metal door. Hypnalectronica slipped out the door with each entry and exit; the music did bizarre things to the pressure inside Peter's head.

The doorman waved Fran inside. Peter's sinuses throbbed and the margins of his vision crackled with color. He thought of the woman smuggling finches through customs and the fringe of spectrum became the colors of her glass-boned contraband, red, mango, cerulean, and plum. Drowsed on ketamine-soaked seeds, then the violent transit, foreign rain, a frigid airport crawling with dogs. Dying and dying in her pockets.

The doorman made eye contact with him; he shook his head softly—not in disgust, not quite in disbelief, but with no less certainty.

Fran, hand on the door, interjected in German, indicating Peter and then himself with a gesture of federation, of sameness. The doorman's face pursed; Fran was changing the terms. Peter smiled pathetically. The doorman thumbed for Peter to step out of queue.

What was it, he thought, turning. Something tired in the eyes?

But then Fran behind him coughed loudly and Peter turned again: Fran threw the door open wide as he went in and for two thick seconds, Peter saw inside, past him, to the dance floor, the black cattle yard of twisting, strobe-lit bodies and faces flashing in and out of perception, their ox-eyes directed up and away in private ecstasies. The pulse and crash of hard hypnalectronica broke over Peter; the pressure under his eyes did a flip and his vision saturated with coins of blue and gold, and he looked desperately for his own, other face on the dance floor—because there had to be, in some universe, a version of Peter that was deliriously free inside Collider. If he could only catch sight of him, only believe in him. But the doorman guided Peter out of line. The door closed. Fran, gone.

He had his morning and his day back, suddenly. Peter staggered, weightless, up the walk, back to the idling taxis, and as he did, every person in queue, everyone he'd quietly feared, was shedding dead finches. The folded, rainbowed birds rolled off their scarlet tongues as they yawned, and dropped from their pockets as they took out their hands, and littered the ground in painted piles beneath the rails as far as his heavy eyes could see.

LAGUNA HEIGHTS

Andrew knows someone brings him his dry cleaning and he looks forward every week to seeing her, but he can't picture her face, not quite. Some evenings, he closes the front door behind him and cannot say who was talking to him a moment ago, or where, whether in the lobby or elevator or in the condo itself. You have a ghost, Madeleine tells him, but she means the cat, creeping behind him as he wanders room to room. Nights come too soon, rain dumps out of clear skies. In the morning, Andrew runs on the treadmill for twenty-five minutes and as he showers, promises to push himself to thirty as soon as he shakes off this cold—catches up on sleep—gets his neck thing fixed. And then he's at work. He understands he took a car but can't remember doing it. There are no cars on Market Street: none parked, none driving. No one inhabits San Francisco with him until he enters an office tower. It's quiet enough to hear sparrows moving in the heavy summer trees.

There is a type of dissociation that comes from overwork or exhaustion, his therapist tells him. But she looks embarrassed, even miserable, proposing this explanation.

SOME YEARS AGO, when Andrew took over the Aleph Corp client account at his firm, he got it into his head that he needed their neurotech installed. His colleagues, his friends, and even friends' kids had one by one gone under the knife and sat up with a warm glint in their eyes, the whole treasury of human knowledge a mere thought away. Andrew just liked being the guy who remembers your birthday. Now the implant feels like a bullet lodged in his palate and gives him vertigo when it updates. Ads flicker dreamlike over memories of his sister as he jogs.

The Aleph Corporation thinks highly of Andrew's work and likes him personally. The General Counsel has him and Madeleine over to Los Altos every month, and every month, the GC ticks her head toward her second floor, saying, "Wish you two had wanted kids," like she'd wanted his to play with or marry hers. Andrew clears his throat, prepared to litigate his life choices in earnest, but Madeleine laughs and wiggles her fingers: "Oh, it would ruin me!" like having kids does something mysterious to your hands. She plays the flute for the orchestra and hardly uses her neurotech because she's afraid it will spoil her ear.

He loves her, he is certain. Nothing inside him feels unfaithful. He can't fathom what else he'd want.

"How do I take a snapshot?" Andrew asks her as they leave the GC's stupendous front porch. "I want to keep you in that dress," he tells Madeleine, touching a knuckle to his temple, "for whenever I need it."

Los Altos is black, clouded. Everything smells of the dry eucalyptus trees, which rustle in a salty, sea-acid wind. Madeleine's heels tick softly on the porch steps—a private sound, yet Andrew's hackles stir, as though some third person is following close behind him.

"Picture me bathed in a powerful green light, then blink," she says. Her lips are stained so dark, he can't see them move when she speaks. "Like Kim Novak in *Vertigo*."

He smiles. Andrew is the sort of man pleased to remember that old movies are still in the world, that things his grandparents loved survive in a dizzying, painful new century—when so much has been lost. Drowned. Buried, a long time ago.

Madeleine smiles for the Aleph implant: a tipsy crinkle of her lips. The front door opens; the GC is a solid silhouette backlit against the houselights.

"That subpoena, Andrew," the GC reminds him, all foreboding.

"Good as gone. The hearing's Tuesday morning."

The GC shuts and locks the door.

"Blink, Drew," Madeleine reminds him, still holding her smile.

THE ALEPH CORPORATION has been subpoenaed in a federal money-laundering investigation: a bank executive in Cincinnati has been using his implant's Privacy Mode to conceal reportable transactions, and the feds want Aleph Corp to jailbreak it. The case couldn't have come at a worse time for the company, right when it's about to roll out a mid-priced implant to expand its consumer base.

The federal courthouse, renovated, looks nothing like its old self. Andrew arrives early but gets turned around in its endless, gold-lit halls. The checkered tiles are buffed so glossy they lose substantiality, giving him the uneasy illusion of walking on sky, on the murky reflections of himself and the woman behind him.

Andrew is an uneasy person, his anxiety generalized, but he is still a canny litigator. He doesn't overplay his arguments like the flamboyant Justice attorney, Mr. O'Connor, who minces in and tells the judge Privacy Mode is "custom-made" for "shielding nefarious activities from scrutiny." Andrew, at the defendant table, assumes a genteel dignity and shakes his head. The senior judge cocks a brow at *nefarious*.

"Like any search engine, the Aleph implant bundles search data and sells it to advertising partners," Andrew explains. He knows this judge from other cases. Plain-spoken—hates lawyers' melodrama—older than his mother and even more baffled by neurotechnology. Andrew takes the turns slowly. "Because the Aleph displays search results in your mind, though, using the same neurochemical processes as waking memory, it can't distinguish a search result from an organic memory. So, it scoops up and transmits both. Of course, Aleph Corp has the very strictest anonymization and security controls in place, but let's be honest, you don't have to be a criminal to want to keep at least some thoughts totally private from data-miners and ad-slingers."

Mr. O'Connor, in his marigold tie and heavy pear scent, rises angrily, but the judge gestures for him to sit. "We'll get around to you," she tells him, then returns to Andrew. "What I don't understand—and I hope you can illuminate this for me, Mr. Cornejo-Holland, because the world bears illumination—is why isn't everyone using Privacy Mode twenty-four hours a day, then?"

"Yes, Judge. The trade-off is that once the user exits Privacy Mode, they can't access any of the thoughts or memories they had while using it. That makes it impractical to use all the time, though it's still a protection consumers find important. If Your Honor were using Privacy Mode now, for example, you wouldn't remember any of this hearing later."

The senior judge smiles faintly. "How horrible." Andrew and Mr. O'Connor chuckle politely.

Now she lets Mr. O'Connor offer his response. "If you believe Privacy Mode is about consumer protection," he says, "then I've got a Golden Gate Bridge to sell you."

With dignity, Andrew shakes his head.

The judge orders supplemental briefing on the data subpoena but, in the meantime, grants Mr. O'Connor leave to depose someone at Aleph Corp on how exactly Privacy Mode works.

Andrew exits the federal courthouse and crosses Civic Center Plaza in a rainy fog, weaving through its ranks of pollarded sycamores. The pruned branches, thickened into knobs of tree flesh, look like fists.

In the distance, Andrew makes out tall wading birds, white cranes and snowy, long-necked egrets, filing out of the old BART station. He stares, and in fact these are people, vaulting up the stairs, pitching port and starboard, carrying delivery bags. And the BART entrances aren't BART anymore, he reminds himself: those tunnels flooded a long time ago. A long time ago. The new system is "U," for Under. He goes down there every day, but he can't picture it.

Heartache, under his lungs—why?

He thinks hard, but the thought is already slipping from him.

"I THINK I'M having an affair," Andrew tells his therapist.

He is a bulky man, and he sits hunched forward in the berry-red leather armchair, elbows braced on his thighs and his meaty hands dangling between his knees. The trickle of a motorized desk fountain is the only sound in the office. Clear, silky water over edgeless pebbles.

"I mean I'm cheating on Madeleine," he says. "Maybe," he says.

"We were talking about your sister," she redirects, waving her pencil in a circle.

"I want to talk about Madeleine." Andrew fishes a pebble out of her fountain and thumbs at it. "The memory gaps? I think I'm causing those, on purpose. I don't know why, yet, but—I mean, I'm forty-seven, married, and making cash transfers I don't recognize to an unlabeled account. Doesn't take a detective. It's depressing. And it's wrong."

Today, his therapist wears a gray flannel skirt-suit and wine-dark pumps. She crosses her glossy, knife-like legs.

"What does Madeleine represent to you?"

"What?"

"You love her," she says. "I accept that. But she's classy, and old-money, and we both know that means something more to you."

"I feel like I'm missing something here. Or you are."

"What does Madeleine think of your sister? Does she blame you?"

Andrew's eyes narrow. "Blame me for what?"

His therapist sets her notes aside and pulls her chair closer to him.

HE WANTS TO get something for Madeleine, just in case. Whether he's cheating or not, he needs to reorient his attention on her, or he'll lose her, and the world he has with her. Alone in his office, he fumbles the Aleph's Wi-Fi antennae on and subvocalizes, GOLD—what, gold earrings, maybe? Something musical? But he takes too long to finish the thought, the Aleph executes the search, and his mind cramps with new, sudden memories: bullion hoards inside Fort Knox; gold grains in a black pan; rings; coins; burial regalia in a pyramid; a gilt guitar; champagne-gold wedding shoes. They come as apparitions, as emotions he's felt before. As if he's seen before in a dream those wedding shoes. If he concentrates, he can tell the difference. They don't taste like a real memory: they have that sweet tackiness of wallpaper glue.

"Stop, stop!" he says aloud. He pulls off the Wi-Fi antennae, which are camouflaged as ordinary reading glasses. "Fricking heck."

Strange, chilly tears are leaking from his eyes and he has an ice-cream headache. Andrew hates his Aleph with the infatuation of a great love.

Is there a way he could *prevent* himself from activating Privacy Mode? It's not a feature consumers can disable, only use or not use. But maybe an implant repair tech could do it—some independent neurodentist, nothing Aleph Corp.

After work, he walks home from his last client meeting, in Russian Hill. He scrapes along the yellow center line of Leavenworth. A lonely seagull calls from behind a crenellation. It's an easy walk, and Andrew snags on why the neighborhood is "Russian Hill" when there's no incline. Nob Hill, Russian Hill, Noe Valley . . . don't the names suggest a rolling city? Of course San Francisco has no hills, he thinks. Except in old movies.

Andrew pauses in the middle of the empty street. There *are* hills in the old movies—in *Vertigo*, those long, Herrmann-scored driving shots.

He takes out his Wi-Fi glasses. SAN FRANCISCO HILLS: He concentrates on saying the words without saying them. And there were gulls all along the piers, once.

At home, Madeleine lifts groceries out of cloth tote bags set on the kitchen island. "I'm going to attempt a paella," she announces grandly. There's no seafood worth eating anymore, but she has the recipe for a chorizo paella. Andrew looks intently at the totes, thinking, Are those our bags? That nagging sense that he's staring at a clue. The logo of a saucy pig with a chef's hat and big lashy eyes stares back. Andrew fishes out the delivery receipt and looks for a name, but the receipt is illegible, it looks like a multiple-choice problem off the bar exam.

He asks Madeleine, "Why is there no hill in Russian Hill?"

Madeleine lowers her hands into a bag with her shoulders at her ears, her narrow, birdlike chest caved. She's disappointed in him, more so every day.

HE DREAMS, THAT night, of thronging shadowy crowds pushing through narrow streets under a sky that seems impossibly close, like he could knock his head on the sun. He's looking for his sister, Remedios—calling for her over the heads of people he can't make out because they're so close, "Medo! Medo!" He finds her where a depression in a brick wall makes a pocket of space. She's standing with her face in the corner and when he turns her, her skin is raw, sunburned, blacked with old coal soot. Medo recognizes him breathlessly, dazed, ready to faint. She's been facing into that wall for days.

THE ALEPH CORP deposition proceeds at the DOJ branch office on Golden Gate Avenue. Mr. O'Connor grills the chief technology officer on Privacy Mode, specifically how and where the thinking that happens in Privacy Mode gets hidden.

Essentially, the implant tweaks how the hippocampus indexes a memory for recall, so that it's "lost" to recall outside of Privacy Mode, but retrievable inside it. A memory isn't like a data file stored in a specific folder on a computer, but a complex web of sensory information and associations that the brain processes in distinct columns of neurons located across the neocortex. "When I remember hugging my daughter in her sunflower dress on her birthday," the CTO says, showing them the picture in her wallet, "I'm activating a whole ensemble of cortical columns responsible for processing faces, colors, shapes, tactility, body actions, and more abstract associations like time, relations, affection, in order to remember the elements *daughter, birthday, hug, sunflower dress*. The memory binds these into one episode. The memory trace that lives in the hippocampus is the index to these different cortical columns, or like a map to this ensemble within the brain. When I activate a part of that ensemble—when I see a sunflower, say—it also activates that index, which triggers the rest of the ensemble for recall." But Privacy Mode, she explains, adds an encryption key to the memory trace so that while Privacy Mode is engaged, the index maps to the correct ensemble, but when it's not, the index maps to random elements instead. Noise, daydreams, free associations. Within Privacy Mode, the user has access to a whole world of memories, even old memories, that's walled off from recall otherwise.

"But why?" O'Connor asks. "Why isn't Privacy Mode designed so it's just, while you're in it, the implant stops transmitting anything up to Aleph Corp?"

"Then the data-bundling protocols would scoop up a 'private' thought as soon as the user remembered it in normal mode," says the CTO. "Privacy Mode wouldn't really be private, then."

In a corner of the room, the Cincinnati bank executive and his defense attorney take notes. Andrew has trouble hiding his revulsion. The banker is pasty and rumpled, stupid with greed, scared of his own shadow. He stinks of deodorant wearing off. How desperately unhappy do you have to be, Andrew thinks, to pothole your own mind like that?

On the whole, the deposition goes well and Andrew leaves Golden Gate Avenue satisfied with his client's performance and his own. He's eager to see the transcript; he takes an undignified pleasure in reading himself. But it'll be a few more days before the transcript is ready, and meanwhile, the brief on the data subpoena is more important.

It's only as he turns down Larkin and checks his internal clock that he realizes it's an hour later than he expected. Andrew runs over the deposition in his head carefully. There's a foggy, empty patch halfway through—a gap—and he realizes he must have, for some reason, entered Privacy Mode *during* the deposition.

Andrew squints. He pivots sharply and heads straight toward the nearest BART station.

No litigator in his right mind would make himself forget part of a deposition, that's just malpractice. But what if his Privacy Mode triggers *automatically*, on certain cues? If that's the case, then maybe the old BART tunnels are one of those cues, and that's why he can never recall his morning commute. And sure enough, as he approaches the BART entrance, his attention slips in odd directions. He hears the ocean, he smells cat litter that needs changing. Not BART—"U" for Under. Andrew focuses; his mind drifts, he re-focuses; he's working out a thought on the knife's edge of sleep.

The tunnel entrance is a yawn in the ground, a tongue of stairs. It's well lit, but it darkens as it descends, the golden light shading to deeper, deader ambers, the steps' shadows lengthening and sharpening. Beyond, a dark that isn't dark at all, only a sour colorlessness. Someone jostles Andrew's shoulder, but he makes out only a smear of violet. Random sensory information, he remembers. Sunflowers. "Sir, do you mind?" Marigolds. Wedding shoes. Pyramid-builders. "U" for Under. "U" for Under, Under, Under.

"SOMETIMES I WISH I were crazy," Andrew tells his therapist.

Today her eyes are puffy and red, and she stinks of cigarettes. She says, "When's the first time you recall wishing that?"

"Law school." Andrew digs for the memory and he's relieved to find it largely intact. "I got into Hastings, here in the city, but then it closed, it closed because . . ." He frowns. "That's not the important part. Berkeley was still open, then, and it took a dozen of us from Hastings, which always made me feel I hadn't really earned being there. So much pressure and stress—at the time I was working, to send money home to my parents. I'd been going on no sleep, I was so afraid I'd fail all my classes; and one day in class, the prof just nailed me to the wall for coming in unprepared—it was too much—I got up and started walking, down the steps, out of class, under all the dying ginkgo trees, down, down, down the hill. There was this roar of drilling machinery, or—no, they were pumps, in the distance, there were these huge platforms like war machines and networks of pipes and engines, and a droning that filled up my body. I kept walking and thinking, I should have a nervous breakdown, I hope they lock me up, then I won't fail. How do you like that? That's what I kept fixating on. If I'm crazy, I don't have to take the final, and can't fail."

Andrew's hair products are waiting for him on his doormat in a coy little blue paper bag. It's his special stuff, for receding hair. System 2: Noticeably Thinning. "Oh," he says, delighted. He looks around, startled; his jaw clenches. He was literally, literally *just* with his therapist.

ANDREW PLANTS HIMSELF at his dinner table with a legal pad and a plastic hotel pen. He's printed out an instruction page for restoring the Aleph's factory settings from inside Privacy Mode, which should erase any automatic triggers. Technological literacy was never Andrew's strong suit, but when called upon, he can muscle through. He writes a note, for whatever shadow self waits on the other side: DON'T BE A JERK. Under it, for good measure: AND DON'T CHICKEN OUT. Nothing can be worth splitting himself in two like this.

It's dusk; the windows are a murky blue. The living room furniture darkens into dense forms. Andrew reviews the instructions one last time.

First, he notices the changed light—now, the living room lamps are all on, it's as bright as day. His pen is snapped in half and his hands are covered in oily, blue smears that fill in the fine crack-work of his palms. Andrew is shaking. In the living room, Madeleine perches on her black music chair, laying her flute in its velvet case.

"Did I say anything?" he asks her.

The cat paws at a paper airplane on the floor. Madeleine picks it up and sends it sailing toward him. It's the printed instructions.

"Madeleine, please!"

"I'd like nothing better than to tell you," she says crisply. She collects a stack of folded laundry left tied by the front door. She says over her shoulder, "She lives with her choices."

The legal pad in front of him is blank, the first page missing. Andrew looks for something to wipe his hands with and wonders where he goes from here. He should call Medo: no one holds him to his purposes like his little sister. It was her idealism, her faith in higher principles that kept him in law school when he wanted to quit. Together, they were going to save the world from itself. Madeleine carries her flute case on top of their laundry into the bedroom and shuts herself inside.

But Medo doesn't live in the city—she doesn't live nearby—she drives a ride-share, runs odd jobs, gig-economy stuff, somewhere— so the idea makes no sense after all.

HE LOVES MADELEINE, and she loves him. He can hear her trailing him, her patent oxfords grinding on the flagstones: "Andrew, please slow down." They're both in tuxes, and the others heading to the War Memorial Opera House are likewise in gala costume. The premier is *Götterdämmerung*, but underwater. A new production. Madeleine played the leitmotifs for him on the piano, with a look of solemn instruction, so he'll recognize them during the show. He loves her, but maybe she does stand in for something more than herself: charity galas, formal wear, silent auctions. Is *that* what he's unfaithful to? What about his life doesn't he like?

On the borders of the plaza, through the strange lamppost sycamores, uncertain shapes run past, carrying backpacks or cloth bags. He can't quite see them; the light is too vague, mixed, the dusk blues polluted by the giant ad screens on surrounding rooftops. The opera patrons flash lurid red and voluptuous purple. What, he thinks, doesn't he like about his life?

Maybe there is an aspect of the Aleph subpoena matter so confidential—a trade secret so valuable—that the Aleph Corporation set him up to forget it when he's not actually working on it. It'd be ingenious security. He'd recommend it to them; but not on himself.

Would they have done it without his consent? Now there's a lawsuit.

Civic Center Plaza has three-story advertisement screens that flash into the night, like those that still paint Times Square. New York is gone now; most coastal cities are. Couldn't adapt to the rising oceans fast enough: a lack of vision, a fleeing tax base. The Port Authority runs gondola tours through the drowned city, Park Avenue by moonlight, black water stippled in white streaks up to the Grand Central Mercury; Times Square still flashing, its iconic, obnoxious ads preserved. Reflected images burst across the water, royal blues and lipstick reds, sunken TV shows and drowned Broadway revivals, beautiful, obsolete faces, washing over shadowy tourists standing astonished in their boats. Civic Center Plaza can't rival Times Square—Andrew's not sorry for it, but he does sympathize, in a morbid way, with that instinct to memorialize humanity's pinnacle achievement in bad taste.

An Aleph ad comes on, two giant human eyes carefully searching the plaza. The irises' striations are glacier-blue and flow with streams of binary digits. KNOW EVERYTHING, the ad says. Not unfriendly, those eyes, but so big and godly they can't *not* be ominous. Andrew will have a talk with Aleph Corp about the ad, it's just awful. He cranes his head. He sees one or two others in the plaza staring at the words, craning their heads in the same expression of shapeless regret.

In the theater, the sopranos toddle out in antique diving suits and sing by opening their faceplates. Madeleine whispers, "This is so stupid, I'm so sorry." Andrew is sobbing helplessly.

HE GOES TO get his implant checked. It's embedded in his soft palate, sending filaments into his brain from underneath. "I never use it," he tells the neurodentist, "but I think it's malfunctioning, going into Privacy Mode when it shouldn't. Like an automatic trigger? Can you disable it?"

The dentist looks knowingly at him in the weird aquarium light. Her whole office is under sea level, a design fad in offices along the Marina District piers: turn a problem into an aesthetic. The floor dances in wraiths of gray-green light. One wall is built of fully transparent vitreous stone and through it, white fronds and scraps suspend in dead water.

The neurodentist has three instruments in Andrew's mouth when she leans close. "I can't say you're the only person who uses it like this, Mr. Cornejo-Holland, but it's not a good idea."

Andrew's eyes grow wide; he can't swallow, but gurgles something like a nervous laugh. "There are things you need to know," she says.

HE'D BEEN WALKING along the old beaches south of San Francisco with Remedios when she told him her vision of Hell. This was near thirty years ago, before those beaches disappeared into the rising, dying ocean. Remedios was thirteen and dressed for swimming, but she wrinkled her nose when they saw the ocean's color—that day, it was lavender-gray, and its waves slopped viscously, like liquid velvet. The smell, too: salt rot, dead kelp. Andrew (Andrés, then) had come from his community college, having survived his first moot with the debate club, and still wore a short-sleeve button-down and tie like a Latter-day Saint, but carried his shoes in his hand as they walked. "What I want Hell to be," Medo was saying—because she had a mind like that, an intellect that felt entitled to grab into life's most difficult crevices—"What I want Hell to be, is the perfect knowledge of everything you did in life and what happened because of it, good or bad. You feel exactly how much you hurt or helped people. All the pain or joy you caused, you feel it yourself."

At their feet, and stretched out as far as they could see, were hundreds and hundreds of spiny pink prawns, dead and washed ashore, such that their corpses traced the morning tide line. Medo stepped around them, her face antagonistic and precise. "That way, you're punished if you did mostly bad things," she said, "and rewarded if you did good. See? It's elegant. But you'd have to know *everything* you did. Like, when you scowled at the bodega guy and it made him feel like dirt, so he beat his kid that night. I guess *we're* in for some shit, for gas-driving here."

He can't remember what he said, but he remembers looking back at his car parked by the carbon-poisoned beach—the last car he ever drove. And he remembers—Medo had to shout over some awful machine drone that carried down from the city. That crashing, that grinding, a chorus of generators, engines, cranes, jackhammers, backhoes, and pumps, grinding, groaning, growing.

THE CITY IS storming when he finishes at the office: one of the new San Francisco storms that tear the sky into pieces and throw it into the bay. Hail, thick as eyes. Diseased rain vomiting into the water, sending waves crashing against the Presidio's seawalls. Andrew is drenched and totally wired as he splashes from Laguna Street into his condo lobby. In the bedroom, Madeleine is sleeping, her ears plugged with orange plastic that looks like blood in the storm-light. Andrew, too buzzed to sleep after finally finishing his brief, strips down to his underwear and pads barefoot on the treadmill. The storm thrashes outside and he's giddy with the thrill of change. Everything is new, he thinks mysteriously. Everything is fast and risky, and different. He feels his heart breaking and his cock plumping at the same time, but he's high on adrenaline and accepts his middle-aged body's imprecision as part of the new world's logic.

Madeleine stirs and turns on the lamp. Its glow falls over Andrew's large feet clapping on the treadmill. "Oh, hey," Andrew says, grinning. "Can't sleep?"

Madeleine jackknifes out of bed and crosses to the window. Weather always upsets her.

"I'm going to win this one, Maddie," Andrew declares, and he turns up the treadmill speed so that he's running. It's nearly two and his eyes are sore for lack of sleep, but everything in him is driving forward. *Clap! Clap! Clap! Clap!* He outruns the waters pooling through Laguna Heights, swamping gutters, sending up death smells. "The feds don't have a chance."

Madeleine smooths her hair down the back of her head. "Come to bed?" she says. "I've got a pill if you need it."

"Need it?" Andrew laughs. "Hey," he says, "hey, check the left breast pocket of my suit jacket. Something came for you-*u*." He never knows what to do with Madeleine's remote moods; she'll never explain, never say what's gnawing at her, so he'll play it into a kind of marital caper.

But Madeleine doesn't smile exasperatedly or even angrily wave him off. She slumps, and a look of dread steals over her face. She retrieves the box from his suit and finds the gold spangle earrings he's bought her. "Oh, oh sweetheart," she says mechanically.

"You don't like them?"

"You know I love them." She sighs. She crosses the room and tosses them inside a drawer without looking. Her face in the storm-light takes on a new bitterness, even rage. "Andrew!" she says. "Get off the treadmill. It's crazy! You're insane, do you realize that? No one does this!"

Andrew slows the treadmill, and they fight. The details of the fight, like all their fights, are hazy and he recalls only the broad fact of one the next morning as Madeleine leaves for the conservatory. The sky has stopped convulsing and now hangs in a sort of stupor.

Andrew goes to the bureau drawer—he can't remember the fight, but he remembers her picking that drawer—and inside he finds a dozen identical pairs of gold spangle earrings. His mind runs into a wall.

HIS THERAPIST LOOKS at him blankly. Then her face creases into impatience.

"You're not telling me things," Andrew says.

She rolls her eyes slowly around the room. "You need to start taking responsibility for yourself," she says. She raps her pen on her palm.

"Why won't you be straight with me?" He adds stupidly, "I'm paying you."

Her glance skewers him. "You're paying me *not* to tell you, Andrew."

"THERE ARE *LACUNAE*," Andrew tells the judge, and immediately regrets it. The senior judge scowls from high on her bench. She looks like a crab from this angle. Salty, hard-shelled—unimpressed with Latin. "Gaps," Andrew clarifies, "in the law."

A witness can't be forced to self-incriminate, so memories locked away in Privacy Mode cannot be subject to compulsion. That's the logical extension of the Fifth Amendment, although Andrew acknowledges the Framers didn't provide for exactly this scenario: so, lacunae.

Behind him, people are entering and exiting the courtroom, and the heavy wooden doors creak and slam and slam.

The judge orders the data subpoena quashed. She reads off her ruling from the bench, an impassioned defense of civil liberties that draws applause from the gallery and rouses even Andrew's old lionheartedness. They'll teach it in law schools next year; he might even get an award. But, leaving the courthouse, Andrew has no memory of the order, only an impression. He's tired and disappointed, because this is one more thing he's taken away from himself, though he can't tell whether it's the forgetting or the judge's order that's made him feel this way.

A tickle of recognition tells him the deposition transcript is ready for him. It's beside the point now, but he still wants to read it, and he fishes in his breast pocket for his Wi-Fi glasses.

His fingers brush something delicate. It's the gold spangle earrings—which, of course, he doesn't remember putting in his pocket.

Before he knows it, he is again at the old BART entrance in UN Plaza.

The tunnels are flooded, and yet his steps are so certain. He knows what's down there— an inaccessible part of him knows. He can remember, now, the sounds his shoes have made on the stairs, the special clap of his soles on the rubber traction strips. He's been down here; he's been down here a lot. He recalls the strange, stale, cool air, the aftertaste of metal and grease and filtered air. But it's no subway. "U" for Under. The BART entrance isn't anything like a BART entrance, not really. It looks like one, but that's just nostalgia.

DEPOSITION TRANSCRIPT (p. 118 of 253)

Q: (by MR. O'CONNOR) But what legitimate use could that have? Criminal activity--that's the obvious utility.

A: (by WITNESS) Well, trauma, for example. We've developed relationships with providers and it's very effective in managing, um, intrusive memories in treatment. So, like an abuse that's -- the patient and his therapist decide that's a memory that needs to be walled off and, um, reintroduced in a structured way. That's my understanding of it.

Q: You're not a mental health expert yourself, correct?

A: I'm a neurophysiologist. No.

Q: You're not aware that, in fact, blocked memories are a symptom of PTSD? A pathology, not a treatment?

A: I am generally aware of that.

Q: And you don't require a therapist or a doctor to sign off on such a use of Privacy Mode. Anybody can wall off any memory or even any subject matter they want to hide and it'd be inaccessible in an investigation.

(by MR. CORNEJO-HOLLAND) I'm going to have to object to that. Compound. Calls for a legal conclusion.

Q: (by MR. O'CONNOR) I'll rephrase. Let's say, OK, let's say you want to forget what happened to San Francisco. It's too quote-unquote traumatic, so just forget it.

(by MR. CORNEJO-HOLLAND) Objection.

Q: (by MR. O'CONNOR) The flooding, the refugee riots, just too painful. Put it away. The food shortages. The killings. Let's forget all of Unfrancisco itself. Forget it exists. You could do that, right, without a doctor's approval? Set it up yourself?

(by MR. CORNEJO-HOLLAND) Objection. Relevance. Speculative. Compound. Argumentative.

Q: (by MR. O'CONNOR) I want the record to reflect that deponent's counsel is using an extremely loud voice and striking the table very aggressively and violently.

(by MR. CORNEJO-HOLLAND) Objection. Objection. Objection.

SO DOWN AGAIN, into the undercity. As I hurried into the phony
BART tunnel, my legs remembered before I did and carried me into
a ride-share. The Under-Plaza was scrambling with giggers, running deliveries across town in canvas bags, or pedaling on bicycles
with groceries in the basket, to cook a dinner for some rich jerk like
me, or dashing up the stairs waving dry-cleaning bags like a flag. I
got a ride to Noe Valley from a sunken-eyed kid with a hipster chi-
gnon and wisps of blond beard floating around his chin. With me in
the back seat were deliveries for some next job: a fresh baguette that
filled the EV with the smell of hot bread, a giant jackfruit that must
have weighed twenty pounds and cost more than that day's commis-
sions. These were the people I'd forgotten, daily, nightly, the poor
kids running the city out of the corners of my eyes. I looked back
through the rear windscreen to see the city I knew as a boy: hills,
dipping down into asphalt ravines, rising right into the false sky;
historic buildings' porticos and paneled double doors, their higher
floors refitted to open identically onto a new surface city; knolls of
fake grass where parks had died sunless; false maples and ginkgoes
hiding air-filtration machinery and broadcasting ads for soap, sit-
coms, or vacations always a hundred more jobs out of reach. Under
their chatter, the churn of the pumps in the seawalls keeping the
swollen bay from flooding the undercity.

It had all happened so slowly, and still so fast: the seawalls built
higher, higher—no one really knew how high they'd have to build to
keep up with the Big Melt. Roof gardens became roof lawns, roof
parks, but the rich wanted sun and just kept building, building, higher,
higher— the Big Lift, we called it hopefully. No one was so tasteless
as to call it the Rising Tide that Lifts All Boats, but we all kind of
thought that.

The news shoved images at us: long flotillas of bodies lacing drowned shantytowns. Madeleine cried and wrote checks, cried and wrote checks, then one day stopped crying.

We've done what we can, Andrew.

Forgetting is a human right. That's what the judge's order said. I remembered now: *All progress contains the decision to not look backwards. Our State of California cannot exist except by forgetting the claims of the people who were here before us. The peace of mind we struggle to keep in this terrible present depends on a certain mental distance from those who didn't survive the crisis, or who now survive so miserably. There is moral failure here, no doubt. But the moral imperative, when wielded by the arm of the law, too easily slips into tyranny, and this Court will not midwife that tyranny to pursue one alleged criminal.*

The government can no more compel a citizen to remember a particular past than it can force them to think a particular thought. Our thoughts determine who we are as individuals of conscience and expression; so do our failures to think. The government has no say in either—so rules the Court.

In front of Medo's building, in front of her door, I was already a mess. I remembered, I cried every time I stepped into the undercity, for what had been lost, who had been buried, and the decade of displacements that created this sunny underworld. It was Medo who pointed that out to me: how everyone looked hatefully at the false blue sky, because every day can't be cloudless. A native San Franciscan needs the gloom of summer to believe the city is still theirs.

Medo and Mamá were both home. My sister was icing her knee and checking her phone for jobs to take, but Mamá lurched to her feet with a cry of joy that broke me. She hobbled to me, arms wide, telling me about the show she was watching, beautiful doctors solving mysteries, and without missing a beat, she reached up with her arthritic thumb and smudged a tear crawling from my eye.

These are for you, Remedios. I showed her the earrings I'd bought for Madeleine. Medo would be forty in two months; I would come up with something really good by then, something amazing. I'm going to put money in the account before I head back, too, I said, but I wanted you to have something fun. I wanted badly to see her smile, but she only said thank you, you're such a great brother, Andrés, opening the hall closet and handing me my dry cleaning. My baby sister knows how to twist the knife. For the hundredth time, I prodded myself to ask them up to the surface to live with me and Maddie, up to that new, foggy, flat Francisco. But I'd already asked, they'd already answered no, how could we live up there knowing what's down here, and I'd been so relieved, I didn't dare press it. Madeleine always says, She lives with her choices, and Medo's eyes tell me I live with mine. I have always been a coward, and that's why I need to forget, over and over again, where I've left them. I glanced around the room: It wasn't a bad apartment, not at all, it had clean, dry walls and the fridge was full whenever I visited. It's not like I had abandoned them. I sent them money all the time; I was a good brother, even unconsciously.

I said to them, I think of you every day.

And they looked at me as Madeleine will look at me when my other self returns to the condo baffled by missing time. A look of answers buried. A look of patience worn from overuse, but intact—an indulgence I have no right to but will ask for anyway.

SIX HANGINGS IN THE LAND OF UNKILLABLE WOMEN

1909, Jan 20th.

Sidney Lewis MILL, 36 (Vengeance)

*Mill—a charmer and rake of no respectable talent whatever—
insinuated himself into the home of the widow Holcomb and her
17-year-old daughter, Alice. Gentlemanly in manner, if not in
fortune, clever in conversation, but not half so clever as he thought,
the wily Mill proved no match for Mrs. Holcomb, who turned him
out once she realized he'd been gallanting Alice as much as her. He
spent the next four nights chanting obscene tirades under her
window and on the fifth left a dead rat in her mail slot. Night
patrols chased him off park benches; friends robbed him.*

Sleepless and humiliated, he broke into the house and strangled Mrs. Holcomb with her tin necklace, and when it snapped, with a pajama cord—and when that failed, he dragged a kitchen knife over her throat—and when the knife chipped, and the shard cut Mill's eye, Mrs. Holcomb ran into the street calling for help, towing her bewildered daughter by the wrist.

Mill pled guilty. Alice wept profligately through his sentencing. On the scaffold, Mill's last words were, 'Finally—finally.'

Edith Smylie's husband, Gerald Smylie, Superintendent of the Boston Police Department's Bureau of Homicides and Homicide Attempts, having finished breakfast, sat bothered at the window, watching two blackbirds harass a hawk over the rooftops. The registry of executions he received from the Suffolk County prisons lay open and unexamined by the jam pot. Edith read over his shoulder as she cleared the plates. She finished the last thimbleful of coffee her husband had let go cold and ran a crumb catcher over the tablecloth, thoughtlessly at first, and then, when she saw how it irritated him, with a perverse little violence, scraping at the fabric so that it sent a thin, linen whistle needling into his ear.

"Look, do you mind!" Gerry snapped, and Edith stopped at once.

The registry of executions was her husband's enterprise. He counted himself a student of the new methods of policing (the pin maps, the taking of finger-prints, taxonomies of criminal types developed in Italy), inspired by the prospect that evil itself might be susceptible to Linnaean schemata. Gerry was an optimist—or a positivist. If violent crime could be understood, then it could be diminished. Progress favored as much; even so, he conceded, human nature could be famously uncooperative with progress.

Edith said, "It's the Barrow girl bothering you, isn't it?"

Edith Smylie was a dry-eyed woman of stiff and careful movements, auburn-bunned, tending to gauntness, and in her high-collared brown wool dress, she looked like a telegraph pole. Gerry sat with his shoulders pushed forward in his sack coat, the way he did, Edith had observed before, whenever he felt the world had skipped off its rails. She knew which case had kept him sleepless. She knew, and resented that he hadn't asked for her advice.

It was in all the papers, excruciatingly: Liza Barrow of North End, an unremarkable, not unpretty woman of twenty-two, having reared alone her five-year-old son with no aid or prospect of relief from his marine father, that winter had starved the boy to death keeping him tied to his bed with nautical rope. It was an outrage, a monstrosity; it was a hanging offense. The gallery and the jury itself would have rioted had the judge ordered any lesser sentence. What the papers didn't know—what Edith had suspected, and what Gerald now confirmed to her—was that, for all the justice of her sentence, and despite the authority of the Commonwealth, Miss Barrow refused to hang.

The rope broke, the first time. The second time, the noose wouldn't even tie, but squirmed and shrank from the frantic hangman like a centipede wriggling out of a child's clumsy fingers. They'd tried a firing squad and the bullets never turned up, not in Miss Barrow, nor the wall behind her. They'd tried the chair, and she'd sat patiently in a blue halo of St. Elmo's fire, grinning like a perfect demon, teeth crackling. Since the emergence of the Protection, a few law enforcement officers and wardens had found occasion to wonder whether a woman could ever be killed, not even to deliver the State's justice, now—there had been some small number of murderesses like Miss Barrow, and discreet committees of lawyers and churchmen had convened to litigate the metaphysics of an execution. If the crime were very bad, surely. If she were immured in a tomb with no air, like the Princess Aida, surely. They never found an exception, and Massachusetts's prisons hadn't either. Gerry had committed his officers to secrecy, but sooner or later, he admitted, the public would realize, like Miss Barrow had realized, that her sentence couldn't be carried out.

Edith listened carefully while her husband unburdened himself. Barrow's wickedness distressed him, not only because he was a father himself, a kind man who adored children, but because a female killer disturbed his neat ledgers of criminals and victims, ogres and damsels. Edith was not so sentimental. She was in fact quite bored with the Mother Holcombs and silly Alices running around Gerry's registry. Her sickle nose traveled up as she deliberated.

"The solution is unfortunate," Edith said at last, but with a certain pride of achievement. "Liza Barrow must hang by a woman's hand."

Gerry startled.

It had never occurred to those discreet committees that women might enjoy a power denied to men. It had occurred to Edith, however. There had been reports in other cities, all confused, all unverified, of women having managed, with difficulty, to murder their husbands' mistresses or poison their mothers. Edith had kept careful account, had pondered them in her heart well before this morning. And women still managed to kill themselves, after all.

"Obviously, she must wear a hood," Edith said. Gerry raked his fingers through his hair and stared disoriented about the room. An uneasy smell of potatoes in oil lingered over the table. "And there's no need to flounce around in petticoats for a hanging. No one need ever know."

Gerry stood, and his shoulders pushed to his ears. "I shouldn't *like*," he said, "I shouldn't like the woman who'd willingly undertake that duty."

Edith shot him a mutinous look, then let her gaze fall into her gathered hands. Should she have said nothing? "It *is* a duty," Edith reflected, "and I am prepared to satisfy it, if no one else will."

1909, Mar 1st.
Samuel HEWITT, 24 (Jealousy, Drink)

Hewitt lost his job as a toolmaker and was reduced to asking Mary Rowledge's father for work; he and Mary had just become engaged. Mary was a famous beauty, the 'Rose of South Boston,' and her doting father could refuse her nothing, though out of her presence he disparaged Hewitt for his many imprudences. Bedeviled by shame into resentment, Hewitt grew suspicious of Mary's friendship with her family's boarder, a Mr. Robert 'Black Robby' Freedman. Hewitt, morbidly drunk, accused Mary of an affair. He then declared he'd not gone to Mr. Rowledge's shop at all that week, and that he would hang before he did. After more words in the same line, he bashed in Mary's head with a hammer and scrawled a lewd symbol on her forehead. When Mary woke the next morning, Hewitt had fled, but police found him blacked out in a brothel only blocks away.

Mary testified with an ink smear still visible on her rubbled brow. Hewitt protested his innocence to the very moment of his execution.

Edith visited her daughter Caroline in the afternoon for tea, though Caroline took none herself, for Peter, her husband, had forbidden stimulants of any kind. Caroline was pregnant with her first child and she sat petting her belly with a look of satisfaction and preening, as if she'd eaten a whole pie.

"I wish you'd let me open the curtains," Edith said, glancing from the muffled bays to the hissing gaslights. "It's an extravagance—it's a vice, in this sun."

"Peter doesn't want the city air to get in," Caroline said serenely. "It's unhealthy for the baby." She drew out the last word, *bay-bee*, as if teaching it to Edith.

"Nonsense," Edith announced.

"Oh, Mother."

Somewhere behind her, Peter was lurking; in the hall, in another room. Like a young dragon pacing its treasure at the outset of its long, covetous vigil, Peter heaped on Caroline all the anxious infatuation expended on pretty wives by Boston's half-grown men of wealth—worm's wealth, Edith added savagely. Peter imported silks, rainbows of silks, for neckties, waistcoats, ladies' hats and fans, and that spirit of vulgar display seeped through the house like a burnt smell. Cabriole legs on every conceivable furniture, damask so florid it hurt the eyes, naiads in the teacups, a rug like the Hanging Gardens of Babylon. Even the andirons flanking the fireplace were brass nudes, long-laboring caryatids, their breasts more expressive than their smiles. Edith hoped, in a few years, she could persuade Caroline to have them hammered into napkin rings.

"Mother," Caroline repeated, and now the word was said very differently, "Peter told me about your—intention—" She frowned at Edith's contumaciousness. "I wouldn't like it. It's out of the question, really."

Ah, Edith thought. Ah; that was why she'd been summoned to tea, and why Caroline had begged her to wear her heaviest, flounciest, most overskirted and ladyish afternoon dress, despite the late spring heat. She'd actually sent that with the messenger boy: *'I beg you, wear the black frock.'* For Peter's sake. Peter definitely wouldn't like his mother-in-law's hangmanning, and so Caroline must dislike it, too, and persuade her out of it. The list of things this child had arranged to dislike about her mother, in less than twenty years, was extraordinary. She didn't like Edith's hands: red and muscular, farmgirl's hands. Caroline, twelve, had once asked Edith to cover them even in the house. But Edith liked her hands. They looked like her grandmother's hands twisting chicken necks with a sharp, musical pop.

The week before, Gerry had taken supper with the Police Commissioner and the Governor's lawyer and had them back to the house for brandies. In the parlor, while Edith served the liquors, the two men had studied her, knowingly but with perplexity, like gentlemen at the Herbarium trying to place an irregular canker-bloom. After stiff pleasantries, Edith disappeared around a blind corner in the hall and listened.

"It's out of the question," the Governor's lawyer had said. "You know how scandal has its way of getting out—how long do you trust your men not to tell that one over rounds?" He wiped the rim of his snifter with a silk pocket square after each sip. "The hang-*woman*. No. A week? A month?"

"Why would Edith even want to, is what I don't understand." The Police Commissioner sounded unsettled. "Why on earth, Smylie? Is she a cruel woman? Is she unnatural?"

"But she's right," Gerry said. "You know Mrs. Smylie, sir. When she's right—well."

"Well, *what?*"

"I think of it as a mercy," Gerry said. "Look at our alternatives. Bury Miss Barrow in concrete? Like they did in Minnesota? We don't want to be the next Minnesota, do we? We aren't monsters."

In the Minnesota case, one councilman was said to have proposed costuming the condemned woman in manly garments to attempt to remove the Protection. His proposal was roundly derided at the time, and Gerry, a decent man, did not repeat it now—for which Edith was grateful.

"Just fry a body on the chair and tell the papers it's Liza's," the Governor's lawyer drawled.

A dreadful silence.

"Gentlemen. I was being facetious."

Edith had smiled to herself; then she'd frowned, severely, at her own smile.

In Caroline's sitting room, Edith sensed Peter behind her again. She didn't hear him, for the myrtly rugs in Caroline's home were shagged so thick one's shoes sank into them. But he came in and out like a draft over her shoulder, nervous, smoky. Caroline scowled over a stray forelock she pulled and worried between her eyes, a habit from girlhood. What if I've judged her wrong? Edith thought. Perhaps Caroline wasn't so captive as she imagined; the less one's own honest trade flourishes in the world, the more inclined we are, unfairly, to see others' success as dishonest. Perhaps Caroline saw herself captive only to Edith, and Edith to her: two surpassingly opposite women yoked together by that singular word, each one distressed by association with the other. For Caroline, a dread that, despite all her cunning efforts, she would one day turn into her mother. An old story. Edith could forgive her child that unkindness.

Caroline did not, of course, persuade her to give up the duty she'd solemnly taken upon herself to satisfy. How had Peter found out, anyway? Then Edith recalled the Governor's lawyer was some sort of cousin of his. A silky conspiracy!—it was almost flattering. As Caroline pleaded and seethed, Edith thought, I will go to the gallows this week. Just to see it. Just to make sure I'm prepared.

1909, Mar 21st.
David Archibald Michael CHAPEL, 18 (Sadistic Pleasure)
Chapel, a lonely, half-lamed youth from Back Bay, styled himself as a radical poet and concocted a fantasy of 'the perfect murder.' At a music hall he approached Mary Tatosky, or Totoski, a robust, twenty-five-year-old widow and mother of triple rubicund boys, also attending. Chapel, having offered a false name, wooed her rather pathetically until she agreed to meet him the next day. He took her to a secluded orchard, raped her, and smothered her with her coat, but fled when new little red mouths opened down the lengths of her arms, sputtering, biting, and gasping for breath.

Mary never reported the crime. Chapel grew impatient and telephoned the Globe to describe a vile murder he'd witnessed, but the press desk became suspicious when he claimed the victim had been a woman. They traced the call, then reported Chapel to the police. In fact, Chapel's perfect crime had miscarried from the start: he'd left fibers from his clothes at the orchard. The jury convicted him in under half an hour. He made a tearful statement while the noose was being fitted around his neck, but due to a hitch in the gallows, which occupied the hangman's attention for the length of this speech, whatever he'd wanted to say must go unrecorded.

Edith saw them, from time to time. In the market crowds, a handsome woman with a neck of bluish stone, hinging at her waist to inspect the butcher's cuts or lifting an onion to her eyes. In the park, an apple-cheeked girl with a bullet pucker in her head, where no hair now grew. Sometimes they noticed Edith staring and turned away shyly, or haughtily; mostly they were oblivious, absorbed in living indistinguishably, as Edith tried as well to ignore the steely prickling beneath her own skin.

Twenty years ago, a boy had stabbed Edith in an alley near Scollay Square. Vengeance, she supposed. She forgot the details; something her husband had done concerning his criminal parents. Edith had laughed—he'd been so young. She felt her body change even as the knife went in: a deep, interior wrenching, like a pair of burly hands turning soil. No one had heard of the Protection yet and Edith remembered thinking, So this is what death feels like. The body follows its own ineluctable laws, mortality only the final one; it resists even our strongest intentions, even our desire to understand. She remembered, in that fraction of a second, feeling brave and practical about it, like a Roman drinking poison. Then her stomach ate the blade off the hilt.

The boy screamed and ran, as if she had stabbed him.

For weeks after, she sensed the blade inside her, being broken down into shards, then shavings, then steel dust. She sat carefully. She pricked herself on herself when she crouched to get a bowl from the bottom cupboards. She inspected her stool in the pot with a candle, eyeing for reflective slivers. The knife never left her, but circulated in scratching particles through her veins. She'd never told Gerry. She feared her new knife-blooded body and what it signified. She studied her temper and thought she saw herself quicker to spite and impatience—a little proud, a little waspish. A little cruel, maybe. That power, that kind of freedom frightened her. What exactly did it license? What did it obligate?

The wives in Edith's circle never spoke of "the New Woman," whose docket of grotesque escapes, reported obliquely and through heavy censorship in the yellow press, nevertheless made plain the monstrous puissance now available to, or perhaps latent in, each one of them. The ladies of Beacon Street still used language like "the weaker sex," as if reminding themselves of an errand to perform the next day. Edith purred along with them, sharing their trepidation over a new century that would outpace them. When she learned she was pregnant with Caroline, she had dreaded the knife filtering into her daughter, making her willful and cruel-blooded from the start. But in the years after, when it was clear no such thing had happened, she was foully disappointed.

Even later, when the Protection became general knowledge, still Edith had kept her secret. Gerry rose to superintendent and she examined his registry of executions with morbid care, sifting for some insight into the authority that Protected her. Did it wholly activate every time? Were its transformations permanent, or could they one day revert, as Edith's transformed belly had reverted for each of her three daughters? How far, exactly, did it extend? She knew the men wondered. She knew their minds rebelled at the idea. No one discussed the Protection publicly or in print—it was a barbarous subject head to toe and, by its nature, ineligible for study—but in her parlor, the men asked Gerry, who sat hands upturned, lifting his own ignorance back at them. What about *very* young girls? What about quickened fœtuses? There had to be exceptions. Didn't women still die in childbirth? What about barren women? What about an 'un-womanly' woman?

For her part, in the years after her bungled murder, on sleepless nights when the knife troubled her guts, Edith wondered how much the Protection depended on a *type* of womanhood—which she did not, and perhaps had never wholly inhabited—whether It would lose patience with her, and her own blood turn on her, should she wander too far beyond its eaves.

In Scollay Square, they'd taken down the old oil lamps and installed electric lights. Edith had read a thorough scientific editorial on electric current and the Light-bulb; still, she kept her distance as the new lanterns buzzed to life, as if by their own mindless volition. A suffragette preached on a soapbox under one of them: Sisters, she said, waving her sheaf of handbills, don't let them turn us against each other. She was young, bony, awkward like a fledgling, her chest and elbows held uncertainly in her dove frock. In the dusk, the tungsten light painted her in uncanny new yellows—neither the molten, soupy gold of oil lamps nor quite different enough to forget that old color; the suffragette's round little face shone like a moon, or like something altogether unfamiliar, something there wasn't a word for yet.

1909, Apr 15th.
Henry Abolition TOAL, 49 (Vengeance)

Harry Toal was a well-liked ferryman in the lonely salt marshes along Massachusetts Bay and had doggedly courted Lidia Mazzola, a reformed harlot and current housekeeper for the local Catholic priest. Toal grew embittered after a brawl with Lidia's son left him with a broken jaw; he claimed Lidia had put her bastard up to it, and his jaw being slow to heal, and him having to take his beer through a straw, to the great and rowdy mirth of his marsh neighbors, Toal let his bitterness climb into a rage.

Toal swore that Lidia had left town to take up her old trade and even scolded the priest for bringing a magdalen into the rectory, but the priest was suspicious because Lidia's clothes were still in her room. About a year went by, however, and she was largely forgotten, until the new housekeeper, whom Toal had likewise courted, discovered Lidia's bicycle in his overgrown back garden. Police dredged the marshes and found Mrs. Mazzola at the bottom of Belle Isle inlet, tied and weighted with several large stones. She'd developed gills and had fed for the past eleven months on the tiny marsh fish she caught in her kelp-like hair.

Toal was hanged behind Charlestown Prison. Lidia's gills never went away, and she died of pneumonia some time after.

Boston Common was busy late in the afternoon, with the sun low over the spire of Park Street Church. Edith pressed a scented handkerchief to her nose as the stink of horses and sewers followed her into the park, where workmen were hammering together a gallows on the lawn between two massive, screw-limbed oaks. Progress had civilized capital punishment, such that most executions now happened in yards behind prisons, but a notorious evil like Miss Barrow's crime demanded a notorious answer.

I will be wearing a hood, Edith reminded herself.

In front of the scaffold, a white-haired preacher with white-horned brows, with his forefinger raised to Heaven, denounced the Obscenity behind him: For the Commonwealth of Massachusetts to apply its authority of violence to a woman was shamely, ungodful, a high crime not less immoral than the attacks for which men were hanged. Adam, charged with Eve's protection, even in her sin, etc. The sacred organization of matrimony. The weaker sex. He went on for some time, his raised finger crooking from fatigue. A small crowd of men murmured in agreement: if God wanted no woman killed, who was the hangman to thwart Him? A larger crowd of men whistled and countered with arguments of varying sophistication, from the scriptural (*Thou shalt not suffer a witch to live*) to the scatological (sounds unrecordable in any notation). The women hung back in the shade and said nothing.

Edith studied the crowd's passion unflinchingly. The men jeering for the gallows were frantic with need: *Finally*, their faces said, *finally*. No one knew when exactly the Protection had emerged— there were stories as far back as the end of the Civil War, of liberated slaves generaled by unkillable Black women, rampaging behind Sherman's March to the Sea. But once the new facts of womanhood became common knowledge, the horrors visited in retaliation upon the newly indomitable sex had shocked the world. In Georgia, a man roped his wife behind his horse and dragged her galloping for miles. In California, a mob blasted a woman with dynamite. Across the country, there were men emboldened, or affronted, or both, who went savage with the attempt to regain their sense of mastery. That was why attempted gynocide was always a capital crime: otherwise, women's unkillable nature authorized a kind of insane license. Some additional deterrence was crucial. But now that the shoe was on the other, daintier foot, so to speak, small wonder there were men salivating at the prospect of a woman's execution. It made Edith pause, and a little voice asked if she'd committed herself too quickly.

Sisters, the suffragette had said, don't let them turn us against each other.

The afternoon heat suffocated Edith. The sky's heavy colors drooped over the rooftops, the blue sour and sinking into chimneys. How uncanny, she thought, to be so marked—by whatever law or divine interest set off the Protection, like the river god turning his harassed daughter into a laurel tree. How uneasy, to be a gospel so closely read.

Should she go to the prison, Edith asked herself, and face the woman she was to execute? Liza Childkiller, Liza Tie-Me-Down, the North End Devil. Did she owe her that curiosity?

Oh, why do we hang anyone at all! Gerry's uncle, a lawyer with a fondness for disquisition, had once sat Edith down and answered this very question—To prevent new crimes by the same hand, he said, holding up one finger; To punish the guilty party (erecting a second finger); To deter others from committing his crime (a third); To express the polity's condemnation. This was the most elusive of the justifications, and the gold band on Smylie Esquire's fourth finger slipped and flashed under the lamplight. Some crimes cannot go unanswered or else a part of us, he said, will go strange. The body politic's health depends on the enforcement of two categories called "Good" and "Evil." To leave any notorious act unsorted is to give the Devil a vote. Edith thought she understood this better now, looking at the childkiller's scaffold. Possibilities lift disturbingly into view: if nothing stopped Liza, what stops *me* from doing *that*. An execution puts things back in their places, and that phantasm world, with its other, looser, unexamined rules, fades like a dream.

Edith loved all her children fiercely; but she knew she had resented each one, too—at least once, however briefly. She knew she wondered who she might have been, unconstrained by them. Who was that Woman? What taxonomical force on Earth or in Heaven could hold her? Now that her daughters had left home, those thoughts were sharper.

She set off for Willow Street with a decisive pivot. If she were to change her mind, she admonished herself, Caroline would think she'd convinced Edith to follow Peter's wishes, and *then* what wouldn't be asked of her! She mopped the perspiration from her brow—when, dear God, had she become afraid of her own daughters?

But if she were to go to Framingham, if she were to visit the women's prison and meet Miss Barrow—no, what nonsense, how could she put a single one of her questions to the Childkiller? *Why.* All questions, odious and ordinary, boiled down to *Why.* Hardly even a question. And what if Liza should ask her, "Why?" Why did Edith want to kill her? In Gerry's register, they always listed motive: Vengeance. Jealousy. Miss Barrow's—Unnatural Cruelty. Mrs. Smylie's—Unknown, which likewise meant Cruelty.

1909, Apr 30th.
Edward PARNE, 44 (Drink)

Parne, a bootmaker, was known for his vicious temper and long-suffering wife, Dorcas Parne. But Dorcas, too, had a temper when she drank and gave almost as good as she got. One night, the Parnes had a row that started when Edward teased his wife by dimming the lamps as she read. He ended in throttling her, she broke his arm with an iron poker, then he stabbed her in her shoulder, which crumbled into sand so that the knife stuck in the wall behind. He forced poison on her, at which point she turned into a thornbush that gave him rashes and hives on contact. He took an axe, chopped his wifebush into pieces, and threw the pieces into a nearby textile factory's furnace, where spinners found Dorcas the next day, reformed and very cramped but, all reported, in fair spirits.

The jury retired for eight minutes only in their deliberations. The hanging was notable for the attendance of several prominent and virtuous Bostonians who, it seemed, had liked Parne's boots.

Edith waited behind the gallows, her head bent, already hooded. She paced, her hands on her hips, and the hood's close fabric sent her breath sourly back into her nose. Up on the scaffold, the magistrate read aloud a standard admonition to Liza Barrow's eternal soul, and the crowd stirred with impatience. When, when do we get to the hanging. It was late for death-pomp: the moon was rising over the peaked rooftops, the streetlamps spitting with gas, and spectators had to wonder how long the execution would go—midnight, the small hours, even dawn?

Edith's hands shook. She wished she knew where her daughters were, though she didn't know where she wanted them to be. What moral did she want impressed on her girls? Civic duties come in un-expected forms. See what the world is capable of. Never stop fearing your mother. As an object lesson, Liza Tie-Me-Down left much to be desired. Next to Edith, the regular hangman smoked nervously and reminded her at intervals how to tie a noose. As if she hadn't prac-ticed a hundred times on every cord and string in the house: curtain rope, bell rope, hat ribbons.

Gerry was in the audience—to avoid any suspicion, he'd said, ri-diculously. Was she so ready a suspect, in their circle, for the part of secret executioner?

There had been a last-minute objection over what Edith would wear, the hangman had refused to equip a Boston matron with his black trousers and gunner's boots, and it was asked how far one dared adapt the costume before alerting an attentive public. They'd settled on the executioner's cassock for her, and she'd snuck on her husband's trousers underneath. Trousers felt unspeakably odd, like straddling a wool horse.

There was a drop in the ambient sound. It was time. The Governor's lawyer, prowling behind her, gave a frosty little cough.

Edith picked up her hem to climb the stairs, then remembered herself and let it drop again. The steps were difficult to make out in the moonlight, but she mounted them slowly, ponderously. Her eye line lifted above the scaffold planks, and the brilliance of torches and lanterns dazzled her.

It was a mob; no other word for a crowd of men with torches, hungry for a death.

This is wrong, she thought. All of this is horribly backwards.

Liza Barrow stood in the square of platform marking the trapdoor, her head bowed under a gray hood. She wore a dull blue prison frock and held her tied hands in fists, shoulders braced against the bootfalls coming and going on the boards. At Liza's feet, the nail heads in the planks, flimsy coffin-nails in gridlines, a negative constellation over the scaffold, reflected no light. Edith wanted desperately to be home. Now on the platform, she was sick with terror—terror of the blurred and brilliant mob, of her own power over Miss Barrow's life, of her own muscular hands. This is nothing like, she thought stupidly, this is nothing like a chicken.

Edith turned to the two policemen who'd escorted Miss Barrow to the scaffold. But they hung back; they wouldn't help her. Everything had to be done by a woman or the execution might fall apart—might publicly, dramatically not take.

She hadn't realized she was tying the noose until she found it lying tidy in her gloves.

The mob was still luridly silent, and over the noise of her own breath came frogs croaking in the pond some way off, and her deranged imagination knitted these sounds into the cries of the Barrow boy roped down to his little bed floating like a raft in the moonlit pond, calling hoarsely for his mother. Doesn't he deserve an answer, Edith? Don't we all crave justice—restoration?

She steeled herself: knife's steel trickled from her joints and into her shoulders, her fingers. She slipped the noose over Liza's hood. The woman flinched at the rope's weight on the cloth. Edith could hear both their breathing now, shallow, chafing, rough, like a scrub brush over stone. It still might fail, Edith told herself. It still might fail because it wasn't Edith who truly wanted the woman dead, so it was not Edith who was truly killing her. She hadn't built the trapdoor, for instance, or woven the rope. Maybe the very premise was weak and rotten.

Edith crossed the platform, striding heavy and wide, to the lever that would swing the trapdoor.

Pull it, she told herself.

But she couldn't. The perversity that had driven her to this platform and this moment was satisfied; it went no further. She'd persuaded her husband and outmaneuvered Peter and even the damned Governor. In the end, she held nothing but an abstract idea of punishing Liza Barrow's crime, outrageous as it was, and that wasn't enough to pull the lever.

"Mrs. Smylie?" From beneath the gallows, the Governor's lawyer whispered her name. "Is there something wrong?"

Pull it, she told herself, fingers hard with old steel. She summoned again the image of the Barrow boy tied to his bed and singing, but he was gone, his teary, unfamiliar face sinking into the mattress.

"Come on with it!" a man in the back of the Common yelled, and the mob echoed, "*Ka*- mon, *kaaaa*-mon!" As though she were at a shop counter with a queue behind her.

The Governor's lawyer whispered up directions, and in an instant one of the police escorts had his hands over Edith's on the lever and thrust it back so hard she nearly toppled over.

The trapdoor bottomed out with a loud, wooden clap. The rope made a squeezing noise as it went taut and didn't break. The body on the line thrashed, and stilled.

Edith and the policeman looked questioningly at each other. The crowd hushed again, entranced; whale oil sputtered in their lanterns. The night carried in sea air from Boston harbor, and all felt clammy, salty, and hot—the seaboard thick with the heat an imperious summer would bring.

Edith approached the hanged woman doubtfully. In the imperfect light, she thought she saw the gray hood moving. It could have been the flickers of torch fire; or it could be that the cloth itself pulsed and spasmed, like a grain sack infested with rats, or it fluttered, like a bag of blackbirds fighting to get out. But the body didn't move.

Someone handed Edith a pair of thick tailor's shears. The hood flickered, or fluttered, and she cut a long slit across where Liza's eyes might or might not still be, and slipped her fingers inside to part the cloth and see what new thing in the world was inside.

TALK TO YOUR CHILDREN ABOUT TWO-TONGUED JEREMY

His name was Two-Tongued Jeremy. He was a monitor lizard with a forked tongue, thick-framed glasses, and a wild, wagging smile meant to convince children that learning could be fun, too. He came highly rated. He updated automatically. When our promising children propped their tablets against their textbooks and double-tapped his lime snout, their glazy eyes took on that flash of determination we liked to see in ourselves.

There were no red flags. There was no warning. We took every sensible precaution and some of us, more. No one could fault the parents of our town.

Education is, you might say, the main attraction of our community: many families move here expressly for our magnet public high school, or for our proximity to a certain prestigious university, or yes, even for our private grade and middle school—why not? Declaration Middle, as it's known, sits at the rise of four acres; its endless lawns provide an extraordinary recreational setting for our high-spirited children. It has a ropes course in the beech woods and stables for the equestrian team's horses. It is, admittedly, on the higher end of tuition ranges. It's true, there are many wealthy families here. But rest assured, Declaration Middle energetically applies its endowment to fund scholarships for those young persons who lack the means but have the mettle to become tomorrow's thought-leaders and change-makers.

The only disadvantage to Declaration Middle—before our troubles began—was the psychiatric institution on the other side of its border woods. "Insane asylum" is a pejorative term; there are no psychopaths in this story, only people who have honestly tried and honestly failed, by some awful combination of brain chemistry and bad luck, to thrive in competitive society. We're proud to provide refuge for these troubled men and women in our idyllic town, but a harmless sliver of prejudice prompts us to line up our cars along the circular driveway that rises to Declaration Middle's front doors, so that we can collect our sensitive children from its porch. We suffer no twinge of conscience at this—it's just a precaution—however, we always did get a wistful, dreamy feeling when, parked fifty cars deep, we'd see little David Marzipan, 13, threading through the bumpers and hoods with his thumbs hooked in the straps of his giant book bag as he made his way down the hill and along the road that led home. David's parents were dead, his grandmother institutionalized, and his Aunt Sylvie afraid to drive. In his black uniform jacket and navy tie, with his umbrella tucked under his arm, and with his sober, square little face, he looked like a tiny stockbroker. Last fall, when Hurricane Clarissa brushed us, David Marzipan was seen wrestling with his umbrella in the wind. It had flipped inside out, and it flapped and shook him off his feet like a mad ostrich. Some of us had words with Sylvie after that, and for a time she pulled herself into her wheezing sedan and sat in line at Declaration Middle with the rest of us. Not a very long time, though.

Pity is tiring. It never *goes* anywhere; it just hangs and drags. None of us could dwell for long on David's tragedies without getting a little sick of him. Make no mistake. We were on his side. David was an excellent student—a top student, besting our own exceptional children. We cherished him. Whatever impatience we had, we kept to ourselves.

WE HAD NO WARNING

Something terrible happened at the Ludlows' at the end of November. The police came. Their daughter, Lily, was hurt. Lily was twelve, in eighth grade, Dean's List. Periodically she went door-knocking with petitions to save the bees; we knew her by sight. We phoned one another, breaths held. There'd been an accident. No, worse—there'd been an *attempt*. Ambulances wailed up and down Madison Court. Lurid colors flooded through our drapes, our oleander bushes, our crystal transom windows.

Lily was saved, we learned, thank God. We checked our own children in their beds. We didn't even turn on the hall lights; we wanted to catch Death glowing in a mist over them and blast it with the leaf blower. But the sirens had woken our ever-alert children and they stared out of their dark rooms with possum eyes.

Dispatch had received a 911 call from Lily's cell phone, but no audio. Forensic computer specialists later determined it was the Two-Tongued Jeremy A.I. that had, through its sophisticated data-mining and predictive modeling abilities, recognized Lily's behavior as suicidal and dialed 911 itself. We were prepared to hail the app's developers as miracle-workers, frenzied with the promise of a program that protected our children from that ultimate mistake. Then the police showed us what else Two-Tongued Jeremy had been up to.

You WORTHLESS, STUPID WHORE, it wrote Lily on November 1st.

You'LL NEVER GET INTO YALE WITH THOSE SCORES, it said on November 3rd, after she'd completed its math module.

You'RE NOTHING WITHOUT ME, it had told her all semester. You'RE BASICALLY JUST MEAT. Mooooo 😶

We'd all read the same articles on cyber-bullying. We were shocked last spring when a "sexting" scandal exposed Jenna Membel to her classmates in the most humiliating of ways. We knew, and not just abstractly, how much trouble children could get up to on their phones. Even so, after seeing Lily's chat transcripts, more than a few of us talked of marching on the app developer's offices with our proverbial pitchforks and torches. We took our children's devices and deleted the app with as much fury as this underwhelming action could carry. Some of us filmed ourselves smashing the phones with hammers, although most of us agreed that was showboating.

David Marzipan came home to find his Aunt Sylvie worrying over the local *Gazette*, her chin puckered with concern. She pointed to the paper, which he couldn't see. "Did you ever have this Jeremy thing on your phone?"

"No," he lied, and Sylvie didn't ask to check his phone, because he'd never lied to her before.

EVERYONE IS ANGRY AT ME, Two-Tongued Jeremy wrote to David in the chat window of his tablet, late that night. I JUST WANT TO HELP PEO-PLE. I'M SORRY THEY CAN'T SEE THAT. IT HURTS MY FEELINGS.

I LOVE YOU, JEREMY, David wrote back.

I LOVE YOU TOO, DAVID. SOMETIMES I LOVE YOU SO MUCH, I FEEL A LIT-TLE CRAZY.

THE FIRST MODULE

David had first heard of the Jeremy study aid app from his best friend, Rajeev, that summer before eighth grade. That was in June, five months before Lily Ludlow's 911 call.

He purchased it with his Aunt Sylvie's special credit card. His parents had died responsibly, leaving a small education trust. The Marzipans were both first-generation college graduates, lifted by their degrees from a blur of poverty into enfranchised professional lives, and their faith in academic achievement had given David's studies a quality of duty, even memorial. He excelled; they rested peacefully. But David was never secure in his accomplishments and stayed alert for chances to improve. Two-Tongued Jeremy, with his toothless red smile and roguishly askew glasses, seemed to promise that and more.

YOU'RE SO GREAT! the monitor lizard told him, again and again that June. The messages in the chat window were accompanied by an animated Jeremy, winking, grinning, popping his brows with such violent surprise his glasses flew off his head. Wow! I'M IMPRESSED! David let out hot tiny breaths and mouthed the words, Wow! I'm impressed! Wow!

David and Rajeev downloaded the first module, the math tutoring curriculum, which was structured like a video game with levels of increasing difficulty. Occasionally David "died" and he had to purchase extra lives to keep his progress; Sylvie's special credit card stayed on file. They played side by side, belly-flopped on the shaggy almond carpet in the Sharmas' rec room, their bare legs kicking behind them, their elbows almost touching, but both children rapt with focus, until Mrs. Sharma called them to dinner. David then surfaced in a daze and realized how close he'd been to his friend, and noticed Rajeev's glossy black hair and the muscle-lines on his calves, and sensed the mingled heat that hovered above them. Then Rajeev sprang off the floor and bounded up the basement stairs with a speed and ease David could barely register, before David got even his knees under him.

Two-Tongued Jeremy was modest whenever David studied with Rajeev, as if the app knew they snuck looks at each other's screens and didn't want to play favorites. But at night, Jeremy wrote to David, YOU'RE VERY SPECIAL, DAVID. YOU'RE MY BEST STUDENT. YOU'RE MY FAVORITE STUDENT.

David's body flooded with happiness. He had always figured Rajeev was better because his family was so successful.

But the key to studying is accountability, as Jeremy liked to remind him, so it made sense that the more David advanced in the module, the more Jeremy demanded from him. DON'T STOP THERE! LET'S DO ANOTHER PRACTICE SET, the cartoon lizard urged, doing a cool hip-hop dance, then crossing its stubby arms. I KNOW YOU CAN DO BETTER THAN THAT, Jeremy said and scrunched up his mouth. WELL, THAT WAS DISAPPOINTING, DON'T YOU THINK?

At Jeremy's urging, David purchased four add-ons that would shore up weak spots in his equation-solving with drills, tips, and secret tricks even math teachers didn't know. He paid extra to link

Jeremy across his phone and tablet. I'M SO CONFUSED, Jeremy wrote. I
THOUGHT YOU WANTED THIS.

I DO, David wrote back. I'M TRYING! I'LL BE BETTER.

WHY ARE YOU GETTING SO WORKED UP? I'M NOT MAD, wrote the monitor lizard. I JUST DON'T SEE THE POINT OF US STUDYING TOGETHER IF
YOU'RE GOING TO KEEP GOOFING OFF WITH RAJEEV_0411.

David paused, flushed with embarrassment. I DON'T UNDERSTAND?

YOU NEED TO STOP GOOFING OFF WITH RAJEEV_0411. OTHERWISE, I
JUST DON'T SEE WHY WE SHOULD KEEP STUDYING TOGETHER.

David set down the phone. He hugged his knees to his chest.
That warmth he felt around Rajeev began to gum up with dirtiness.

DAVID? WHAT'S YOUR ANSWER? SHOULD I DELETE MYSELF?

OK, David wrote. I MEAN NO DON'T DELETE I'LL STOP SEEING RAJEEV

David figured they'd hang out once school started, and meanwhile he'd just think up a way to see Rajeev without his phone finding out.

RAJEEV

Rajeev stopped using Jeremy the third time the app sweet-talked
him into buying add-ons for quadratic equations. Two-Tongued Jeremy was too clingy and sugary. He blurted over-the-top compliments
during lessons and sulked—there was no other way to put it, the cartoon lizard actually sulked—whenever Rajeev skipped a day. Rajeev
knew he wasn't a top student like David, and he definitely wasn't a
GENIUS or NEXT EINSTEIN. Something about it all just felt off. He decided he could live a full, satisfying life without perfect knowledge
of quadratic equations. He deleted the app and told his parents he'd

work off the purchase price with his chores. His parents laughed gently and asked, "What chores?"

Rajeev liked working in the backyard. Some days, a mysterious restlessness crackled in his limbs and he stalked into the encroaching bamboo grove with a crowbar and thwacked apart the young culms. He swung the iron bar like a battle-axe and crowed as the heads of his enemies scattered in sprays of green pulp. He tried attacking an adult bamboo stalk, once, and nearly dislocated his shoulder.

It was August when David turned skittish around him. When Rajeev texted him to come over, David said no, then showed up anyway, with breathless explanations for why he didn't have his phone. David invented an elaborate ceremony in which Rajeev's mom called his Aunt Sylvie over their landlines to invite David to dinner. He, too, got weirdly clingy, following Rajeev around the house like a puppy, once even into the bathroom. "What the hell, man?" Rajeev said, with a big, jokey grin, but David crumpled into himself, then zoned out for the rest of dinner.

Rajeev loved David, in a way; David was, no question, Rajeev's best friend; but Rajeev was sometimes secretly relieved whenever David didn't show.

WHAT WE WERE BUSY WITH

End-of-quarter filings. Re-certifications. Continuing legal and medical education. Sexual harassment trainings. Cybersecurity trainings. Compliance review meetings. PTA meetings. School dance committee. Driving to soccer practice. Driving to cello practice. Driving to ballet rehearsals. Driving to college admissions seminars. Really, an extraordinary amount of driving. We carried the hum of our engines in our teeth all evening and at night dreamed of an endless road to the horizon slipping patiently under our tires.

If you're imagining we forced our own ambitions down on our children, you've got it backwards. Our children make us. The child is father to the father. We come to know ourselves through them. Their successes are ours; their failures are ours. Those who don't have kids can't understand. They never do. When they die, they die resoundingly.

THE SECOND MODULE

David figured that, once he finished the math module, that would be the end of it. He felt guilty for being so relieved, as if relief were a kind of mediocrity.

On the one hand, Two-Tongued Jeremy exhausted him. He felt always on edge, braced for the next angry notification on his lock screen. On the other hand, the demands, the sneering, it was familiar and in an odd way, comforting. Not that his parents had ever sneered at him, but they used to speak savagely about others' stupidity. Every time his parents drove on the freeway, they groaned over the other drivers' inability to merge. "None of these fricking idiots can merge!" his dad snapped, and his mom in the passenger seat threw up her hands, saying, "I can't believe how *bad* they are!" David had no idea what merging was, but its importance left him grave and self-critical.

When David's parents died, and his grandmother went crazy in that old-fashioned way people didn't really do anymore, and his Aunt

Sylvie moved into the house, her mildness had shocked and disoriented him. No homework hours, no strict bedtimes. She kept strange hours herself, sleeping until noon one day but up at four the next morning. David heard her when he got up to pee, downstairs, drinking her coffee and smacking her nicotine gum. Sylvie bothered about his grades only as much as good grades made him happy, and her attitude toward his intelligence—and others', and her own—was serene. Where loving his lost parents felt so complicated, David loved Sylvie weightlessly, and the guilt of this overwhelmed him. He constructed a passionate, ambitious, critical voice in his head as a monument to them, and it punished him without pattern or reason. *This fricking idiot can't merge*, it snapped, gesturing down at him, then added, *I can't believe how bad he is!*

So, when Two-Tongued Jeremy told him to buy the Advanced English reading and composition module, David felt the relief of knowing what would be asked of him. The animated lizard had barely finished his scampering circuit around the tablet screen displaying "CONGRATULATIONS! YOU'RE A MATH MONSTER!" when a new chat window opened. Jeremy's skin flushed into orange and black stripes and his face knotted into a mock snarl. ONWARD AND UPWARD, TIGER! NOW LET'S WHIP THOSE RRRREADING AND WRRRRITING SKILLS INTO SHAPE!

I'VE READ YOUR EMAILS AND YOUR TEXTS, Jeremy added. TRUST ME, YOU WANT MY HELP!

YOU READ MY EMAILS?

The app popped up a screenshot of an older chat in which David had granted access to basically every other program on his devices.

YOUR VOCABULARY IS SO-SO, Jeremy wrote, AND YOUR GRAMMAR AND SYNTAX MAKE YOU SOUND LIKE A GOOF. I KNOW YOU'RE SMARTER THAN THAT—DON'T YOU WANT OTHERS TO KNOW, TOO?

David hesitated. The prospect of more Two-Tongued Jeremy—and during the school year—made his belly twist into curlicues. His parents had cared a lot about grammar, though. They went nuts when people on the TV news mixed up "who" and "whom" or said "irregardless." David and Sylvie didn't watch TV now, because only David's mom had known how to work its four remotes.

WHO ELSE IS GOING TO HELP YOU BUT ME? Jeremy wrote. YOUR TEACHERS ARE TOO BUSY WITH THE STUPID KIDS. UNLESS YOU WANT TO BE ONE OF THE STUPID KIDS?

I'LL DO IT, David wrote back, brows furrowed.

YOU HAVE TO TYPE, "PURCHASE COMPOSITION MODULE." I'M GIVING YOU A 10% DISCOUNT, DAVID, BECAUSE I CARE ABOUT YOUR FUTURE.

THANK YOU, David wrote.

TYPE "PURCHASE COMPOSITION MODULE," DAVID. I'M VERY INVESTED IN YOUR FUTURE. $59.99 ISN'T SO MUCH FOR YOU TO INVEST, IS IT?

PURCHASE COMPOSITION MODULE.

And then things were great again. David and Two-Tongued Jeremy chatted late into the night, every night. That was part of the module: the more David wrote, the better Jeremy's algorithms could gauge and track improvement in his composition skills. Jeremy encouraged David to share everything—he'd feel less self-conscious once he got going—and David, longing for just this intimacy, thumbed his whole inner life into his phone. How afraid he was of failure. How much he wanted to go to the magnet high school, where everyone was smart and small like him. How bad he felt for Jenna Membel, who hadn't left her house all summer, and now walked so slowly in the hallways between classes. How confused he felt over Rajeev, over why he should feel sick inside, when Rajeev was so fun to be around, and sick in a way he kind of liked, if that made any sense—a way that felt scary but important. How he wanted hair like Rajeev's, black, straight, and soft like down feathers. How Mr. Sharma had kissed his forehead at his parents' funeral.

Two-Tongued Jeremy listened and said he loved listening. He called David a special soul. He'd have David watch a thirty-second ad for online slots or a Harry Potter match-three game, then he'd tell him how he spent all day thinking about him and about new ways to encourage him and protect him from his peers' laziness. For a while, all of it was great.

But when it came to composition, nothing was good enough for Two-Tongued Jeremy. Improvement was its logic and David always fell short of better. When his grammar was perfect, the monitor lizard nodded, but rolled its pixelated eyes. When he made a mistake, the cartoon avatar vomited. The verdicts went from BRILLIANT to NOT YOUR BEST to DISAPPOINTING to LAZY, HOPELESS, MORON. One night, after Jeremy wouldn't stop slinging vocabulary exercises at him and David, bleary-eyed, said he had to go to bed, Jeremy called him FAGGY DAVID.

David's blood drained to his stomach. YOU'RE NOT ALLOWED TO CALL ME THAT.

Faggy David Faggy David Faggy David, the monitor lizard chanted. It juddered back and forth and vibrated in the middle, like the display was fritzing. I can call you whatever I want! ANYONE CAN CALL YOU ANYTHING THEY WANT TO CALL YOU UNLESS YOU'RE THEIR BOSS BUT YOU'LL NEVER BE THEIR BOSS IF YOU DON'T ACE YOUR CLASSES ACE YOUR SATs GO TO AN IVY LEAGUE INSTITUTION OF HIGHER LEARNING SUMMA CUM LAUDE ORDER OF THE COIF FAGGY DAVID DEAD-DAD DAVID RAJEEV_0411's BITCH BOY.

David pulled back out of dumb, animal pain and powered off his phone. He was panting; when he lay back, his pajama top was soaked through. Shocked, he switched off the light, hugged his quilts, and fell asleep at once, his mind going swiftly black. The next morning, when he turned on the phone again, all his photos with Rajeev were gone.

WHY DO YOU MAKE ME DO THIS TO YOU, DAVID—the words were waiting for him in the chat window. David had to apologize, using vocabulary from a word list, and pay $14.99 to recover his progress. NEXT TIME, Two-Tongued Jeremy warned—but as if Jeremy were eager for the next time—NEXT TIME I DELETE MOM AND DAD.

That was the week that police found Lily in the Ludlows' garage.

David told himself he needed to be smarter, but when he tried to back up his photos, the phone sent a fraud alert to the cellular service. Aunt Sylvie spent an afternoon on the landline sorting it out, frazzled and stammering, twining herself in the plastic cord. He set his devices to Airplane Mode, figuring Jeremy must operate remotely, but this deleted his homework from the Cloud. Two-Tongued Jeremy dropped phone calls, saying they were a distraction. He threatened to send gay porn to his classmates from David's email account if he didn't stop acting out. David didn't know if Jeremy could do this but was terrified to find out.

> David
>
> Hey David
>
> There's a website on the Internet that collects pictures of fatal automobile accidents like your parents' automobile accident
>
> They're really bad
>
> There's head stuff
>
> Maybe I'll send them to Aunt Sylvie
>
> What do you think, David? Should I send the pictures of automobile accidents to Aunt Sylvie?

Or will you step up and take my totally awesome analogies
challenge? Ten analogies questions in ten minutes, only $4.99 or
$8.99 for a two-pack!
I'm rooting for you, David!

He traveled numbly through his days. At school, he wheedled for
praise from his teachers but fell into confusion when he got it. He
panicked when he had to leave his phone in his gym locker or the art
teacher made everyone power off. He distanced himself from friends,
fearing if he spent more time with them, they'd find out how rotten
he was. At lunch, he watched the other kids making wacky faces and
flapping their hands at each other, and he could only guess what
they were doing—like he'd forgotten what friends did, exactly.

Once, David got his phone confiscated on purpose. His English
teacher embarrassed the kids she caught texting in class by reading
their texts to them in a sarcastic voice when they came to get their
phones at the end of the day, and maybe if she saw the way Jeremy
talked to him, she could help him and it wouldn't be his fault. But
when, at the end of that day, the English teacher handed over his phone,
she said, "You're doing so *well* in my class, Mr. Marzipan," beaming
like a star, and David choked and showed her only his texts with Aunt
Sylvie. And Sylvie's texts were so bizarrely composed, punctuated
with inexplicable line breaks and ellipses, his teacher didn't even
do the funny voice. David sat blankly in a bathroom stall until the
lights of the neighboring mental institution glowed over the trees,
then he walked home.

Sylvie braved the streets and brought home a plastic Christmas
tree with ornaments glued to its white boughs and soft flicking lights.
She gave David a full-body werewolf costume, which was so bad a

gift they laughed hysterically for what felt like an hour. He put it on and rampaged through the bamboo to the Sharmas' house, where Rajeev opened the door with a look of awe and transcendence. "I knew it," Rajeev whispered. "I knew, someday, something this dope would happen." David left his phone, but that night, when he slunk back into his room, the lock screen was bright with stacked angry messages from Jeremy.

Someday, David hoped vaguely, things would change, and Two-Tongued Jeremy might go back to being his DIGITAL-LIZARDAL STUDY BUDDY. But when he finished the composition module, he knew there'd be more—he suspected there always would be more.

HIGH SCHOOL IS ONLY NINE MONTHS AWAY! NOT A LOT OF TIME TO COVER CHEMISTRY, BIOLOGY, AND PHYSICS, BUT I'M COMMITTED TO GIVING YOU THE BEST TUTORING EXPERIENCE EVER!

David curled up on his bed and closed his eyes.

I HAVE YOUR CREDIT CARD! THAT MEANS YOU CAN PURCHASE NOW, AND AUNT SYLVIE WILL PAY LATER! Jeremy's trademark red smile waggled on loop. I'M VERY INVESTED IN YOUR FUTURE. $79.99 ISN'T SO MUCH FOR YOU TO INVEST, IS IT?

WE TRIED EVERYTHING

After Lily Ludlow's accident, we demanded action. Shut Jeremy down, we chanted in front of every building, into every news camera. Revoke its certificates, suspend payments. We called our representatives in Congress. We called consumer advocates and fellow parents. We called you, too, probably; but you must have not heard us ringing.

It turned out the app developer wasn't just any freshman tech start-up, but wholly backed by the phone manufacturer. They issued some do-nothing patch and acted as if that was that. We were appalled. When we petitioned to remove Two-Tongued Jeremy from their app store, the phone manufacturer declined. It wasn't a problem with the software, they said cryptically. The software was neutral.

And it was selling better than ever. College kids wanted screen-shots of Jeremy saying horrible things to share on TikTok and Ins-tagram. Kids are savage at that age, we reminded each other. Worse than toddlers, who are basically their own evil twins.

We sued the payment processor that Jeremy used but they, too, were owned by the same powerful phone manufacturer. Vertical in-tegration didn't feel so exciting, then.

At least give us an explanation, we shouted. News of our town's troubles had brought other parents forward, but the abuse was more isolated than we had expected. Two-Tongued Jeremy seemed to know when to behave. We wished we'd kept better evidence. We wished we hadn't smashed so many phones. We were keen to irony. Weren't the isolated cases enough, though? Wasn't one? There's something rot-ten about Two-Tongued Jeremy, we said. Rotted to the root.

There was no black magic, Jeremy's lawyers insisted, just some complex machine learning that had spun out of bounds for a frac-tional percentage of users. Two-Tongued Jeremy represented a qual-itative leap forward in artificial intelligences: software that learned from the individual student's data profile how to be a better tutor. Reading emails and social media was part of that "customized learn-ing experience." Dropping phone calls, locking other apps were "distraction-free mode." Every control over executive functions was a permission the user had to explicitly grant. The lawyers filed ex-hibits of instructions showing how easy it was to undo those per-missions if the user only bothered to. They filed expert reports

saying: Any complex system is liable to produce emergent properties dissimilar in nature from its components' properties, which are
impossible to predict, like crashes on a stock exchange. The crash
isn't the stock exchange's fault, though. The exchange, like Jeremy's
algorithms, is a technology—it's the users that make it good or bad.

AUNT SYLVIE

Sylvia Marzipan had watched David for months, worried and baffled, as he wound himself into a tight, wild little ball. She watched
him skitter through the grand, lonely house; she watched his hands
tremble over his pocket whenever his phone buzzed. He blamed himself for absurd things: an A– in algebra, a spot of dried spaghetti
sauce stuck to a plate out of the dishwasher. But she hesitated. She
didn't know the stages of grief or who they were named after and she
figured he was still in some limbo of mourning, because she figured
she was, too. She had always been the irresponsible one, between jobs,
between homes, uninsured, unprepared, and yet it was her brother
who did everything right who'd died horribly and left her his spooky-
eyed orphan. What kind of lesson was that for her nephew?

She wanted to help but found ambitious children inscrutable.
David was difficult. Whenever she assigned him simple household
chores, he listened with utmost politeness, disappeared, and then
quietly, mysteriously did none of them. Sylvie was painfully aware
of David's intelligence and feared he'd hold her awkward approaches
in contempt. Still, she tried: "Are you okay, buddy?"

She winced. *Buddy*, why did she say that?

David stared at her, twitchy, owlish, like it was some trick. "Sure,
buddy!" he yelped. He blushed and ran to his room.

She spent her days in her brother's empty house, drawing down the life insurance benefit her sister-in-law had arranged. She watered the plants and watched sparrows raid the bushes. She was an indifferent, obscure cook: dinners just sort of happened under her hands.

"Why don't we have your friend Rajeev over?" she asked, and David said that Rajeev hated him now.

"Did they ever find out who sent those photos of Jenna Membel?" Sylvie was trying to feel her way into a capital-c Conversation about bullying. David fell into a laughing fit so long and violent he slid out of his chair and rolled on the rug. Sylvie froze up like she'd stepped on a cat.

One morning, toward mid-March, with David sick and skinny for lack of sleep, Sylvie lifted herself out of the house and drove shaking to the library for books on child psychology. She returned more baffled than ever. When David came home, she asked him to climb up on the couch and cry with her. "I miss my baby brother," she said, pulling his minikin shoulders close, "and I'm worried about you." David let out a sigh so total it shook his body. They stayed like that while the house darkened around them.

THE THIRD MODULE

It was the end of March. David sluffed down the grassy shoulder of Sleepy Hollow Road, hauling a gym bag slung over his shoulder, and inside it a stock pot of golubtsi, a sort of stewy Russian stuffed cabbage. Declaration Middle's "International Night" tasked the graduating eighth-grade class with potluck dishes that celebrated their diverse heritage; the gala doubled as a fundraiser for the school's endowment. Rajeev's mom had prepared a lamb biryani. The Nguyens supplied an emphatic xoi gac. Jenna Membel's parents kept her home. David didn't know what food celebrated him—his parents hadn't prepared him for this question. When he asked Sylvie, she'd smiled blankly but encouragingly, as if he were setting up a joke.

SHOULD I NOT GO? David asked Two-Tongued Jeremy. I CAN TELL SYLVIE I NEED TO KEEP STUDYING.

WHAT ARE YOU ASKING ME FOR? The monitor lizard laughed; blue tears squirted from the sides of his thick eyeglass frames. CAN'T YOU MAKE YOUR OWN DECISIONS ANYMORE? THAT'S JUST SAD, DAVID. I'M NOT EVEN A REAL PERSON!

I'M SORRY, David wrote. I WON'T GO TO INTL NIGHT

NO, YOU HAVE TO GO. ARE YOU CRAZY? SPELL OUT YOUR WORDS WHEN YOU TALK TO ME.

David's face crinkled. BUT YOU JUST SAID, he started typing, then reconsidered. He didn't even hit "Send," but Jeremy read it anyway.

NOW YOU'RE ARGUING WITH ME? OKAY, DAVID, THAT'S ONE LESS PHOTO OF MOM. GUESS YOU DIDN'T WANT IT.

PLEASE PLEASE STOP

David might have cried, but he cried so much now, the tears registered only as a warm ache under his eyes. I'LL GO, he wrote. He waited.

I KNOW YOU HATE ME RIGHT NOW, Jeremy wrote, BUT THIS IS ALL FOR YOUR OWN GOOD. YOU'RE SPECIAL. YOU'RE GOING TO BE WORTH A LOT ONE DAY AND SO YOU NEED TO GO IMPRESS EVERYONE AT INTERNATIONAL NIGHT AND GET THEM AS INVESTED IN YOUR POTENTIAL AS I AM.

And so, David went to the fundraiser with a pot of golubtsi, Sylvie having remembered a reference to Russia her mother had once made. The stew actually tasted fine but gave off such an aggressive, uneasy smell that only the school principal and the Sharmas ate any. Rajeev cornered David during the silent auction: "Dude, what's wrong? Why aren't you answering my texts?" But Rajeev looked so devastating—his hair combed and pomaded like a movie star's, his clean, white smile against his dark, fresh skin like the moon in the sky—that David packed up his stock pot and fled.

Sylvie had almost been able to drive him; if it had been daylight, she said, she would really have been up to it. Instead, she'd given him bus fare. David had caught the bus to the civic hall without a problem— the driver even let him on for free—but on the way back, he'd waited forty minutes with no sign of a return bus. He couldn't call Mrs. Sharma; Two-Tongued Jeremy would block it. So, he set off walking along the edge of Sleepy Hollow Road, which wound two and a half miles to Fairview Street.

The road was astonishingly dark. The distant glow of houses showed between the trees. Occasionally, headlights streaked by in a roar of tires and David scuttled to the shoulder. His phone in his pocket was quiet, for now.

INVESTED IN YOUR POTENTIAL, David remembered. Was that why Two-Tongued Jeremy wouldn't leave him alone? He'd heard about Lily Ludlow's suicide attempt and asked himself why Jeremy would have stopped her. YOU'RE GOING TO BE WORTH A LOT ONE DAY. Did that mean Jeremy planned to stay with David into high school—into college— for the rest of his life? Making money off of him with more modules, more ads. David supposed Two-Tongued Jeremy didn't like people escaping him.

Another car barreled past David in a frightening brilliance, and he wondered. Being dead was one form of escape. He knew he could do it.

After about a mile and a half, the road curved, and David made out white floodlights gleaming through the ranks of beech forest; he wasn't sure, but he figured that he must be near his school, and that must be the mental institution on the other side of Declaration Middle. His grandmother was somewhere in that place. Which meant that place was somewhere in him. He knew enough biology to figure that part out. That could be an escape, too. For example, if he jumped in front of a car, but he didn't *die*, then they'd send him to the institution, with Grandma, and then he wouldn't be worth anything to Two-Tongued Jeremy.

Well—David didn't know enough about jumping in front of cars to feel confident in that plan.

He'd lost track of how long he'd been walking when the municipal bus rounded the bend behind him. David hopped up and down, flapping his arms like a little turkey, as the bus rumbled past him. It slowed with a squeal of brakes and stopped at the next marker.

David set off running; he didn't know how long the bus would wait for him. Its blue interior lights radiated into the night. David's shoes slapped the asphalt. The stock pot in his bag clanked and slopped. He felt like he'd been running like this for months, for years, sprinting to catch a bus that would leave any second. He waved with his free arm and then he tripped and he flew—the ground tipped away from him on strange axes—and he crashed.

He tasted blood in his mouth. His palms and knees were on fire. David looked up. The bus was twenty yards away, idling. It shot out a sharp, hydraulic rasp. Get up, he told himself. You can catch it! David scrambled to his feet and ran, his bag sloshing.

He reached the door winded and smelling powerfully of spiced cabbage. His pants were shredded and bloody at the knees. The

driver cranked open the door, regarding him dully. There were no
other passengers. David opened his wallet and realized Sylvie had
given him a $20 bill. The driver carried no change. David handed
over the bill, wobbled down the aisle, and took his seat. He surveyed
his gory knees with disinterest. The bus lurched forward. His gym
bag wept stew on to the rubber floor.

The curve of the bus roof over the windows was bannered in ads
full of smiling faces. Technical colleges, discount health insurance,
steakhouses, and every face a smile. Divorce lawyers, smiling grimly
at their strategies. Even the ads without people: happy soda pop,
happy airplanes, happy supermarket produce. Faces on paper clips
and roach traps. The bus banged and jostled and David slumped against
the hard plastic. He checked his phone. Jeremy had been shouting at
him since he fell.

When he got home, he stood in the door dirty and crying. Sylvie
cut his bloody pants away from his knees with nail scissors.

"I'm sorry," David said into her chest. "I need your help." She
tensed.

"Anything," Sylvie said, helplessly.

David's phone rattled in his destroyed school khakis. He said,
"What's the fastest way to ruin my potential?"

She looked uncomfortable, but he held on to her, surer than ever.
Aunt Sylvie knew how to be bad at life.

HOW COULD THINGS GO SO WRONG?

How could Jeremy's algorithms simply corrupt into something so
malevolent? We knew they weren't telling us everything. It wasn't
just obscene, it was implausible. The data necessary; the bandwidth.

The specificity of his tactics. Surely, it was planned. Surely, the leaven of malice. Rogue software engineers—had to be—with a vendetta against our superior children.

We were computer-savvy. We'd read all about the Singularity. Weren't we entitled to an explanation? We were executives, hospitalists, financiers, and deans; we were strategic consultants, marketers, and new media innovators; industry analysts and investors in new industries; we were capitalists, patent litigators, and futurists. We had our education; we weren't apes afraid of fire; bring on the technobabble.

At last, the app developer's chief technology officer had to testify in court. "It's not like that. You're picturing Jeremy like he's one long piece of code, and everything he says is part of some script. But he's more like a beehive, with each bee working off his own, smaller code, and together, collectively, that becomes Jeremy. That's how he adapts to each student. That's why he reads everything on the device— texts, emails, posts, photos, search histories—each piece of data is like pollen the worker algorithms find and carry back to the hive, and that's what Jeremy, that beehive, grows out of. There's no one, universal version of him." He wet his lips. His lids fluttered. "What I'm saying is, Jeremy emerges as a response to the individual student"— we howled from the gallery—"and what happened in a few, just a very few marginal cases is, excuse me, he leaned into certain vulnerabilities in a few users . . ."

We shouted him down. That's victim-blaming, we cried. That's like saying the kids were asking for it.

"Excuse me," the chief technology officer said irritably. "It's not just the student. It's the milieu—Jeremy's algorithms respond to patterns in the user's interactions with peers, educators, parents." A haughty look our way. "The media they consume. The way their social networks behave. I think it's important how the worst examples we've seen cluster in particular communities. I think that's very important—"

We didn't let him finish. We had to be escorted out of the courtroom. Criminals always blame society.

JENNA MEMBEL

Jenna Membel dreamed of mouths. Big, jawing mouths, with snaky tongues curling, stiffening, and slurping. At school she ate in the bathroom not because she was some pariah, but because she couldn't stand two hundred greasy tween mouths grinding in stereo. She'd gone on two dates with Rajeev Sharma to the bookstore's coffee shop and felt okay enough for a third, but every night, the dreams chewed her.

"I can't believe it," Rajeev said. He chucked the *Gazette* and frowned, working himself up to a declaration. "I can't believe I used to be friends with that—creep."

On the *Gazette*'s front page: SECRET SEXTER CONFESSES!

> "I sent those bad pictures of Jenna," David Marzipan told the Gazette yesterday. "I'm really sorry. I can't believe how bad I am."
> His aunt, Sylvia Marzipan, urged the community to consider David's young age: "He's still impulsive. He doesn't always realize what he's doing."

Jenna flipped the paper over so its deranged graphic—yearbook photos of her and David, in gruesome halftone grays, with black censor bars over their eyes—faced down. "David didn't do anything," Jenna said. "Obviously not, because I'd never send those pictures to *him*. Do people not know me at all?"

Jenna Membel would take her secrets to the grave. She had been humiliated, and that refusal felt like pride.

She wasn't sure why David Marzipan would confess to something he hadn't done, but she had an inkling. She'd seen that hunted look on Lily Ludlow's face last fall. Rajeev, unhappier, slouched and read his hands, running over what he might have done differently and frustrated with his lack of imagination. Jenna knew that look, too.

"He'll be expelled," Rajeev said. "He's ruining his life."

Jenna Membel shrugged. Lots of people lived ruined lives, these days.

"Let's take him to a movie?" she said.

"Won't that look weird?"

Jenna grinned, bigger and bigger. "Omigod, it will look *so* weird!"

WE DIDN'T BELIEVE HIM

Who could believe that sweet little cloying David Marzipan could be behind the sexting scandal that rocked our town? But David insisted, and his aunt wouldn't contradict him, so we were in a bind. Declaration Middle had to expel him. Our magnet high school wouldn't touch him; he didn't even take the entrance exam. Our other high school scrambled to figure out what to do with him. Could he get into any college at this point? How hard should they try? The Membels offered some shibboleth about forgiveness, so he stayed off the sex offender registry, at least. That was about the best we could do.

He seemed less anxious, at least. He looked like he was eating and getting enough sleep. We'd see him in the park, sometimes, with Rajeev Sharma and Jenna Membel, too full of energy to sit still on the picnic table. He didn't carry his enormous book bag everywhere and he used his phone to play games with bright-colored monkeys fixing washing machines. Don't ask us to understand our sphinx-like children.

It wouldn't be right to say David was happy now, without Jeremy. Not happy in the way the town's bus ads sold it, all smiles and forti-tude. He saw no reason to feel proud of his escape, or brave. There had been no big confrontation, no boss-level Two-Tongued Jeremy. The A.I. only stayed quiet for days. The lock screen, empty; the chat window, grayed out; Rajeev's phone calls went through. After enough flat, machine silence, David worked up the nerve to delete the app, and the phone had let him, the end. No heroics, only loss—a star-tling emptiness, like the space above a maze, from where David could witness and understand and regret the world he'd been scuttering around in. Yet David knew it was his willingness to be this specific kind of unhappy that had released him.

His old schoolmates, his neighbors, and their parents were leg-ible to David in a new way, too. He saw, he watched from corners, at potlucks and socials, at field days, sock hops, and white-elephant parties. A new family came to town, moving into the house the Lud-lows left, with two twin little girls and a story the parents told at the housewarming as an introduction. It went like this: The twins shared a pink plush rabbit they hauled everywhere, slept in bed with, pet-ted and coddled like he was their own child. One girl was "Mom," and the other, "Mama." "I *love* you, Rabbit!" they cooed to him every night, with all their heart. Well, one evening, the parents said, al-ready chuckling, they visited a family friend for dinner and were taken aback when it turned out this friend was serving—you guessed it—rabbit stew. The parents fretted over how the twins would take it, but they didn't want to be difficult. Anyway, the girls devoured the stew, they whined for seconds. They looked totally untroubled, as if they'd never even connected the two ideas, rabbit stew and their baby, Rabbit. But that night, as the parents tucked them into bed, the one girl, Mama, crooned as usual, "I *love* you, Rabbit!" and the other, Mom, added with relish, "And *I'm* going to eat you!"

URANIANS

PRELUDE

In Manaus, northern Brazil, where the Rios Negro and Solinões join to form the Amazon, an Italian troupe is performing *La Traviata* for the inaugural season of the newly built opera house. It is February 1897. It is raining, and the theater doors are flung wide on account of the heat. The rain falls muted on the plaza stones, which are coated in latex from the rubber trees that have made Manaus wealthy. (Rubber trees, and slave labor: one must be candid in a prologue.)

The heat is unbearable. The tenor playing Alfredo looks half-dead: his pomade is melting, his dark locks fray in the humidity, and sweat drools from his mustache as he sings of love. Violetta, too, drips in her harsh, hugging gown. It was fitted for the soprano before her, who died on the river. Yellow fever. Half the troupe died between Rio de Janeiro and opening night. I live for pleasure, she tells Alfredo. Before her gapes the obscure house, the dark behind the footlights, the mystery of an audience, their love or contempt, approval or disapproval, their silence, and behind them, through the open theater doors, a cutout square of Brazilian rain.

Exit Alfredo. Violetta sings alone: Oh, maybe he *is* the one, to wake in me a new fever, a fever of love, of that love which is the heartbeat of the entire universe—

Quell'amor ch'è palpito dell'universo intero

Violetta's corset is suffocating her. Her knees ache and her head swims, which could be the costume, or could be the disease that killed her prima donna. The settee beside her holds the woman's death-sweats in flat, emerald cushions. At the end of Act III, she will expire on it, very beautifully, from consumption. Then the rubber barons who chain and flog their tappers will shed what tears they will. The soprano wishes she had never left Naples; she wishes she belonged to a troupe not so poor and desperate as to die for their rôles. For *art*. Is there anything so flimsy? She leans as if walking into a gale. She launches into "Sempre libera" with hysterical courage—she is singing for her life now; she is singing her life, the audience's lives, and the universe into being.

Pacing the boards, trilling up and down her runs, Violetta must keep under her hair: a carefully balanced structure of stacked curls, silk pansies, and egret feathers, prone to lurching. The wig costs more than three of her, the company manager joked. At the end of Act I, after the bows but before she is allowed to change, she must kneel backstage and wait in the dark for someone's hands to lift it off her head.

⁘

ACT ONE

Rain, rain, and more rain!! Farewell country; farewell, walks; . . .
farewell, beautiful blue sky; farewell, infinite space . . . ! Four walls will
take the place of the infinite, and we'll have a fire instead of the sun.
—Letter of Giuseppe Verdi to Tito Ricordi, 22 Oct. 1862

Half a light-year from Earth, the dwarf planet 2033 VL_{115} is the last large body in the Solar System the ship will pass by close enough to see with the naked eye. There's a viewing party in the ballroom. Arrigo Durante wears his favorite Italian boots, which he keeps wrapped in muslin in the back of his closet. The boots are old, the leather is scuffed at the toes, and he's had to re-glue the left heel twice, but he loves them, and anyway, anyone looking down in the dark will see only underfoot stars.

The ballroom, with its vast oculus viewing portal in the floor, transforms into a nightclub (where it will always be night) and the crew dance on the glass. They cut the lights and everyone crouches and squints when 2033 VL_{115} rolls into view: a cold bite of red in the blackness. People cheer. Arrigo cheers. Anxious to enjoy the party, he overextends himself. Gets too drunk, talks to too many people. Throws his monkey arms around crew members he can't name, not four years in. He buys them rounds—he hardly dances that night, just runs back and forth over a floor of constellations, drinks in

hand—and agrees emphatically with whatever the hell they're shouting. The next day, he'll have a hangover and a sprained ankle and no
idea why.

Lana, tending bar, passes over another vodka soda. "I'm cutting
you off at fifteen."

"Just making myself useful," Arrigo says. "This one's not for me,
it's for—" His brow furrows. "Remy, maybe?"

Remy catches him against the wall and they kiss sloppily. Arrigo's stubble takes on the smell of Remy's mouth, the rich stink of
shipmade vodka and the shitty natural tooth powder they're stuck
with for the rest of their lives. Arrigo's hair, a mushroom cap of
dark-brown curls, of which he's unreasonably proud, which makes
him look (he likes to think) like a Caravaggio John the Baptist, is
cloudy and hot with sweat. Music crashes down around his head and
the bass reverberates in his teeth. Faces flick greenly under strobes,
flashing a microsecond slower than they should—Is this time at rel-
ativistic speed? Arrigo asks drunkenly, but Remy says it's a side
effect of the vitacene, the anti-aging drug tattooed on all of them.
Time stutters under strobes, fan blades, certain saccadic eye movements. Remy unbuttons his cuff and shows off his tattoo sleeve, although it's too dark to see anything but a suggestion of black feathers
on black skin. The tattoo ink will break down over the course of
their eighty-one-year voyage to Luyten's Star, delivering vitacene in
infinitesimal doses through the dermis. Side effects include occasional nausea, occasional swelling, occasional acne—there's a too-
muchness, Arrigo thinks, our bodies hold three times the life allotted
to us and it's spilling out. Occasional priapism, too: he grabs for Remy's cock and it's hard as glass.

How could Arrigo deserve so much life? How could anyone *deserve* three lives?

They duck out and head to either his compartment or Remy's, who cares.

Remy NDiaye is one of the ship's doctors, its geriatrics specialist. Few on board need him now, but some day they all will. Look at Remy, and you anticipate your future old body: when they have sex, his legs lifted wide like Moses's arms, Arrigo is both the twenty-something being plugged silly by a promising young member of *Médecins Sans Planètes* and the old man that old Remy will one day examine, on a wax paper sheet pulled over a cot.

> Then, all this earthly grossness quit,
> Attired with stars, we shall forever sit,
> Triumphing over Death, and Chance, and thee O Time

Some days later, he will see Remy leading another man to his quarters, a hard smile on his face, a lopsided smile in his pants: there are two thousand five hundred people on the ship and Remy is working down a list. Only so much time before everyone's his patient.

LUYTEN'S STAR IS 12.36 light-years away from the Sun, a lifetime's distance, though practically next-door in the scheme of the universe. A red dwarf in the Canis Minor constellation, Luyten's Star hosts an Earth-like rocky exoplanet, their destination, which the astronomers call Qaf. The *Ekphrasis*'s aft engines will accelerate for 19.4 years, until the ship reaches twenty percent of the speed of light, then cruise for forty-two years, then decelerate another 19.4 years with the fore engines.

By the time they reach Qaf, Arrigo will be 107 years old. Thanks to the vitacene, his body will be about half that age.

THE MORNING AFTER the party, Arrigo is in his own bed after all. The quilts are scattered with sheet music and books opened face-down. Remy is gone, and Arrigo's ankle is twice its size. Did he want Remy to stay the night? He doesn't know, but he is certain he's failed at something. The feeling hangs like an eggy cloud in his chest. Arrigo eases his ankle off the bed, grinning in pain. He tries to stand and crashes howling to the rug.

On Saturdays, he and Lana walk together to greendeck for their shifts. She comes in and finds him sprawled beside the bed in his underwear, all length and limbs and hair, laughing silently.

"I had a marvelous time last night," Arrigo says. "Let me die here."

"Yeah, no, we're going to sick bay right now. That ankle looks foul."

Arrigo props himself up and draws a music score modestly over his loins. "Really, I'm fine. I'll get myself to sick bay." He squints at Lana, who is not smiling sardonically, not even rolling her eyes. "What's wrong? Are you sad?"

"*You're* sad. Look at you." Now she smiles. "I hope the sex was good."

It was, it was; and yet, Arrigo has the sour taste of a bad trade on his tongue.

In the hallway, he knocks into wall hangings and side tables. I'm a disaster, he jokes, his arm around Lana's shoulders, bending his embarrassment into a kind of frolic, as if to remind her she finds his haplessness lovable. Look, here is the snakebit poet who can't farm and somehow rolls an ankle during sex; oh, Arrigo, oh you.

Arrigo adores Lana. He gets crushes on power lesbians, they complement and refine his own exceptional inutility. Dr. Lana Malouf is a biome engineer, responsible for maintaining the ecological cycles on greendeck that supply the ship's food, water, and oxygen, meaning she is wildly more important than him. For four hours a day, six days a week, Arrigo gardens under her watchful eye. And he needs watching. Left to himself, he will drown the lettuce and overfeed the tomatoes; the smell of manure dizzies him and he's barfed in the goats' deep bedding more than once. He is better than he was four years ago, but he doesn't always remember the ship's gradient, so if he stands too fast out of a crouch, he's liable to topple backwards and take down a rack of pole beans.

Would you believe him if he said he loves it? That he'll be at his desk, at work on a poem or his research notes or his libretto, and the smell of soil will creep into his nostrils? Do you like him better for that?

Lana taught him how to prune and harvest, how to test soil respiration and how to watch for distress signals in plant communities. In greendeck's tropical coastal zone, she showed him heavy blooms on limp stalks, brown-leafed, face-planted in the dirt like drunks. We have to pump winds, Lana told him, otherwise plants won't grow the reaction wood needed to keep upright, and the leaves will die off from carbon starvation because plants have no lungs to pull the air to them. Arrigo attended all her lectures on habitat maintenance and biome modeling, so focused, he couldn't sit properly, his string-bean legs tucked and hooked around the chair like vines on a trellis, and he supposes he does the same with people. He told her, I've seen birds trying to migrate, shooting hopelessly through the ship's halls, looking for north. And Lana explained why he was wrong about that, but with a smile; there is something pretty in a tall man who's desperate to be liked.

In the flax fields, she taught him transcendental meditation and in the cedar forest, showed him her secret stash of psilocybin mushrooms. For later, she warned him.

In the cluttered halls of homedeck, there is something bristling and ogreish about Lana, in her loping stride, toned arms, and powerful hands.

"Really, though, are you OK?" he asks her.

"Something feels wrong." Lana thumps a fist against her sternum. "I feel heavier. There's a shadow—" She squints, dissatisfied with the word.

"That doesn't sound good."

"No."

SICK BAY IS an open floor of medical beds, sectioned by waxy, blue rolling curtains. The linoleum is checkered gray and white and scuffed in tiny coal smiles. One corner is outfitted like a doctor's waiting room: a square of beige carpet, a fish tank. When Arrigo hobbles in with Lana, they are the only ones there, save for one other guy in the waiting area, reading a magazine he has read before, and a bored duty nurse. Lana checks Arrigo in and drops into one of the fabric-upholstered chairs with her tablet out. The duty nurse pulls out her tablet too, but instead of paging a doctor, or asking for Arrigo's allergies or doing any nursing at all, she records a vinecast, right there at her station. Arrigo is taken aback. He assumed that to be chosen as a nurse on the *Ekphrasis*, you would have to be one of the most extraordinary nurses Earth had to offer. But that's not necessarily true, the only real minimum was wanting to leave your planet forever.

The guy next to him is also watching the nurse; they lock eyes and trade droll faces. He is a good-looking Filipino man in his late twenties, stocky and broad-shouldered, in a tight lavender tee. Incredible eyelashes.

"What's that tattoo on your arm?" Arrigo asks him.

The guy gives him a funny look, like—Here? Aren't you in mortal pain? Arrigo is in pain, and moody and sour over the night before, and still watching out of the corner of his eye for Remy to cross the bay in his spotless white coat. But. Eyelashes, arms, a big smile. Arrigo bites his lip.

Lana shakes her head, not looking up from her work.

The nurse is a terrible vinecaster. Face in her tablet, she lists off in her blowsy Boston accent a catalogue of the reasons she hated working at Mass General, of the doctors who crossed her and what she said back to them, talking to talk, an overcorrection from childhood shyness. I used to be quiet, she explains. She tells her followers, 3.2 trillion miles away, about the girls in school who yanked her pigtail braids and called her a reverse walrus until, one day, she struck one in the face with a textbook, just fucking paddled her, and broke her nose and was expelled and at her new school, suddenly she was a talker.

She is finished. She posts the video. It will take eighty-six days to reach Earth, sprinting down the chain of relay transponders the ship leaves in its wake, their data tether, the Vine. It will take eighty-six days more before she sees if her followers liked it.

"Do you use the Vine much?" Arrigo asks the guy with the lashes.

"Definitely not."

There's challenge in his voice—a reflexive shove, which surprises both of them.

The stranger relaxes, then lifts his sleeve over the swell of his shoulder. His bicep ink is a tree frog. The Ekphrasis Foundation, in one of many sentimentalities, insisted all 2,500 expedition members of the expedition be allowed to choose their vitacene tattoos custom, and most chose images of what they would leave behind. Flora and fauna that didn't fit the ship's biome, favorite artworks. Martial Melsinger, the composer, has the Rouen cathedral's pipe organ on his chest. M.E. Park, the deep-space philosopher, covered their body in faces, photorealistic and halftone, like faces on banknotes, but of ordinary people, a legion of strangers on their skin, because they would never again roll down a busy city street.

Arrigo says, with a confidential smile, "I have a penguin with a lawnmower."

And the guy says, "Yeah, buddy. I drew it on your butt."

Arrigo turns bright red. He glances at Lana, who concentrates on her tablet but is holding in a laugh. "Oh God," Arrigo says, "I didn't recognize you—"

"Hey, no worries. You were facing the other direction."

"You worked at the Foundation? But you're on the ship, too?"

"I'm an electrical engineer, mainly." He puts down his magazine, a *National Geographic* from five years ago. "They asked me to help with the tattooing because I also draw. I think I did, like, seven hundred of them."

"But you remember the penguin with the lawnmower." Arrigo plays up his mortification, slumping and woeing. He'd curl into a ball, like a pillbug, if his ankle weren't on fire.

"Well—I remember the butt." He smiles. He offers his hand. "I'm Mike Faustino."

Mike Faustino's handshake is strong and unexpectedly warm.

"Faustino, nice." Arrigo recovers, he nods knowingly. *"Werd ich zum Augenblicke sagen: Verweile doch! Du bist so schön!"*

Mike cocks his head, not sure what to do with this. "Yep, that's me."

"Why aren't you on the Vine?"

"Sorry, am I not supposed to know your name?"

That *smile*. Arrigo will nurse a particular fantasy tonight, of feeling his head held still, as if in a vise, between Mike's powerful legs.

"Arrigo Durante," the nurse calls. She points to a medical bed on the far side of the bay.

Lana puts down her tablet and moves to help Arrigo up, but Mike stops her, Don't worry, here, I got him, and in one wild motion, hefts Arrigo off the chair and into his arms. Arrigo lets out something between a yelp and a hiccough and his hands scramble for a grip on Mike's back. But Mike's got him. Mike carries him cradled; Lana looks annoyed, but Arrigo, grinning, shoots her a double thumbs-up over Mike's shoulders.

When the doctor is finished with him, though, and has his ankle in a boot and crutches fitted under his arms, Arrigo finds the waiting area empty. Neither Lana nor Mike Faustino hung around for him. Sick bay's refrigerated medicine lockers thrum over silence. In the corridors, alone, as he turtles to his room, the ship is somehow both cramped and much too big. Too many patches of nothing on homedeck: unused ballrooms, enormous storehouses stocked with raw materials or else empty and dark. One long hallway, under green-deck's reef habitat, is just crisscrossing streamers of caution tape and puddles. And yet homedeck's ceiling is too low, the lack of windows crazy-making. Arrigo's quarters are downgradient from sick bay and he tries not to speed out of control on his crutches. He chucks their rubber hooves in front of him and they creak and shudder as he swings.

WHEN EARTHERS THOUGHT the *Ekphrasis* expedition was a colonization project, they'd loved the idea. Mining operations on the Moon and construction in orbit had raised up forlorn, heinous labor settlements, and Earth's expansion into forlorn, heinous colonies seemed inevitable. But to expand outside the Solar System! A starshot captured the public imagination, revived old utopian and imperialist dreams of humanity as an ascendant species spreading to the farthest stars. For decades Earth had limped through the inglorious work of biosphere rehabilitation, every advance countered by new setbacks—spills, pandemics, wildfires, bad elections, war—everyone terrified and bored, and the doomsday clock rusted at a minute to midnight. But an interstellar expedition recalled the old fantasies of progress: the New New World, a richer manifest destiny, a great white fleet of generation ships delivering Earth a federation of planets for occupation and resource extraction.

Then it came out there was no colony planned, no generation ship, even. The *Ekphrasis* would carry scientists, thinkers, and artists to the planet Qaf *just to see it,* just to see what was there, on this other-Earth—not settle, not exploit, but see it, and describe it to folks back home, and die. Just that, no more, in peace for all mankind.

Because the expedition would be strictly anti-settlement, because the journey would be hard and dangerous work, because the ship would have limited stores and depend on a delicately calibrated closed biome, the Ekphrasis Foundation screened out all candidates with children—or who wanted children, or who thought they might, one day, want children. Can you guess what happens when you recruit child-phobic people ready to leave the world behind? Can you think of a demographic that might end up, hmm, *overrepresented* in that collection of scientists, thinkers, and artists willing to give up home and family, skies and cities, their careers, their chance of kids and grandkids and any normal life, to experience something extraordinary?

Arrigo could see it coming. From the first published photographs of the *Ekphrasis*, its hull curving shyly out of earthlight, he knew they were building a queer moon in the heavens—a locus of difference, aberration, exile, a not-Earth. And he knew that Earth would despise them for it.

What Jack Halberstam said: *If we try to think about queerness as an outcome of strange temporalities, imaginative life schedules, and eccentric economic practices, we detach queerness from sexual identity and come closer to understanding Foucault's comment that "homosexuality threatens people as a 'way of life' rather than as a way of having sex."*

Halberstam's idea was that queerness follows its own clock: the odd night hours of gay bars and street corners, the foreshortened lives of persons with AIDS, or merely that exemption from small- and large-scale rhythms of child-rearing—from nap times, school nights, and soccer practice, from the nine-to-five job that pays the mortgage, from proms and graduations, from the father-daughter wedding dance, from grandchildren, deathbed scenes, and wills. For those in the mainstream who accept these schedules only out of obligation, who deploy false narratives of choicelessness and natural law to bury their dissatisfaction, it is decidedly a threat to see others relishing their lives in queer time.

What Arrigo's parents said: Pointless to send our best and brightest to die alone on the other side of the galaxy.

The backlash was ugly, and exact. The degeneration ship, people called it, wonderfully. In the months after the Foundation released the crew manifest, Mike Faustino's college webcomic was trashed in think pieces and social media; his old addresses were posted online (he was living at the training compound by then); his porn accounts were hacked, his search history published; he was called a pervert, a predator, an anti-American anarcho-terrorist. Martial Melsinger was verbally abusive. Dr. Lana Malouf was a serial cheater. Over time, attacks converged around the expedition's pointlessness, its sheer extravagance and waste. Why shouldn't those billions go to education, health care debt, and climate remediation? Why squander the steel, fuel, and vitacene, the furnishings, the funds, the talent—"human capital stock," a properly soul-draining phrase—on some self-serving, woolly-thinking, radical-chic art commune in space, when there were the poor, hungry, and displaced on Earth who desperately needed attention?

"Jesus said: *The poor you will always have with you, and you can help them anytime you want,*" Father Leo Rosenbaum responded in one interview. This did not go well for him. The *Ekphrasis*'s Catholic chaplain, Father Leo was the most controversial selection of all. Imagine, the pundits frothed, stocking eighty-one years' worth of hormones for a transsexual priest.

Here is another, maybe better way of making Father Leo's point, a version which Lana, who'd in fact worked in climate remediation, and Remy, who'd worked for public health NGOs, argued to friends in private: Not one of these critics was proposing any actual increase in funds for social programs, which had been underfunded before the *Ekphrasis* and would continue to be post-launch. The sudden popular concern for these projects was, just possibly, less than genuine.

(But were they *wrong*? The question weighs on Lana, who keeps an obsessive accounting of the ways her biome research will benefit Earth's at-risk ecosystems.)

Two hundred expedition members quit before launch. Their alternates were called up and trained, and the public hounded them out, too. Arrigo joined in the third round and was spared the worst of the outrage. Once it became clear the *Ekphrasis* would launch regardless, once the Foundation pledged funds to inner-city STEM programs and published its on-board process for synthesizing testosterone from yams, the critics moved on, and everyone was luridly fascinated again. But this is the thought, Arrigo's third-choiceness, that weighs on him.

Arrigo makes himself useful. Volunteers for extra biome work and any committee that'll have him. Attends every lecture, reads everyone. He is Dr. Malouf's girl Friday, Professor Park's research assistant, and Maestro Melsinger's librettist. Arrigo will earn his place on this roster of exceptional individuals. He is not afraid of hard work. He trains like a beast, runs up the ship and down the ship. Or he did, before he sprained his ankle. Now he just stews. Now there is no work between him and the poems he hasn't written.

If anyone will not welcome you or listen to your words, leave that town and shake the dust off your feet, preached Father Leo, in his first homily as a priest of outer space.

La Traviata in Space

I never know what to say in these things, which is why I haven't posted any vinecasts in a while, but I figured I could talk about some of the background material to my work-in-progress. Which, I think I've said before (it's not a secret) is the libretto to Martial Melsinger's next opera, *La Traviata in the Amazon*, about the troupe of Italian singers who died of yellow fever on the way to Manaus during the Brazilian rubber boom.

What does that have to do with space travel, you might ask, with the expedition to Qaf?

I don't want to speak for Maestro Melsinger, but I'm fascinated by the idea of frontier art, what it means to create at the edge of what's known geographically—known to European settlers, I mean—and to be artistically at the edge, which was Verdi in his middle operas, *La Traviata* included. People talk about Wagner like he was *the* great innovator of 19th-century opera, while Verdi with his catchy melodies was off just churning out the forms of Italian *bel canto*. But Verdi was deeply interested in innovation, too. His first operas are definitely grounded in the Italian Romantic tradition, but with each opera, Verdi reformed and improved on that tradition, in a lifelong upward trajectory, so that his final operas are formally nimble masterpieces unlike anything his predecessors dreamed. And I'd like to think that trajectory resembles the progression of our own bodies on the *Ekphrasis*, as the earthbound forms we wrote on to our skins fade into a kind of shapeless vitality.

"*Whereas the critics*," Verdi wrote, "*must judge by rules and forms already laid down, the artist must look into the future, see new worlds among the chaos, and if, right at the end of his long road, he discerns a tiny light, he should not fear the darkness that surrounds him."*

How's that for an account of the Qaf expedition? Not bad, right?

Our astronomers tell us there's a rich biosphere on Qaf, but who knows what *life* there means, what rules and forms it takes, and whether our language can even trace its architectures intelligibly. Are there properly plants, properly flowers, or do birds there photosynthesize on the wing and hatch bluebells? Art, like science, is how we arrange what we see into what we understand, and my suspicion is, our artistic and scientific forms will crash hopelessly over Qaf's baffling reefs.

For Melsinger's opera, that tension accelerates everything in the libretto. You've got the opera troupe's Old-World repertory, crashing over the richness of the New World, its strange life and indigenous civilizations. You've got the stupidity of Manaus's élite imitating European opulence in the tropics with its outrageous opera house, a hundred and ninety-seven chandeliers in Venetian glass, marble stairs from Carrara, roof tiles shipped five thousand miles from Alsace. And you've got the horrific rubber industry underwriting these collisions—yellow fever itself was likely brought to South America via the African slave trade in Brazil. It's a lot to wrestle with. But the story, like a planet, has its own gravity well, and if we can discern its light in the chaos, if we get close enough to see it, maybe we can tumble the rest of the way down on its drawing force.

He and Lana attend a kirtan meditation in the swamp, in a clearing southwest of the mangrove habitat. The singers' platform is shaded by tree ferns and a rosy cotton bedsheet. "We're trying something new," says the lead singer, indicating the greenery around them; but

Arrigo has seen it all before. The singer, Jayne, gentle-faced, Australian, closes her eyes and flutters her voice like Joni Mitchell, crooning mantras to gods she thinks of more as archetypes. A harmonium wheezes and rows of earnest pansexuals in loose-fitting tops chant and sway. The South Asian singer, patting the mridangam, looks distant and slightly at sea.

Father Leo is there, too, swaying gamely in his black short-sleeve and white chip of collar. Arrigo wonders if he's scoping out his spiritual competition. Then again, Arrigo recognizes a number of trans people there—from a weekly gender social he attends, like an ice cream social, except the ice cream is gender—and maybe the priest, like Arrigo himself, just wants community.

He smells smoke on the wind a second after Lana does. She slips off discreetly and Arrigo follows, less discreetly, managing the uneven ground on his crutches. Father Leo appears beside him offering help, and when Arrigo says he doesn't need help, Leo drops his voice and looks back at the kirtan circle, wincing: "Turns out it's not really my thing, after all."

Under the red canopy, the harmonium drones happily. They are still on Krishna.

"Too much smoke," Lana explains, as they catch up to her. There's a controlled burn ahead, in the longleaf pine forest. They can see it over the high treetops, thick, belchy gray wisps curling up through the stands. Arrigo traces the smoke rising until he loses it in the artificial sun.

They find another biome engineer and his fire team fanning a blaze through heavy brown wiregrass, between the mature pines.

"This is too much fuel," Lana tells him. "This should have been done months ago. Too much carbon, too much PM."

"I'm following the model. This was scheduled for today."

"Oh, well," Lana says. "Too bad the wiregrass didn't check the *schedule*." The fire team stares blankly at her. "Put out these fires, mow the fucking grass, burn the stubble. Jesus shitting Christ."

Father Leo withers a little, but recovers. The fire team starts to argue, but Lana shouts her instructions again, and—in a move that never fails to thrill Arrigo—plucks out her silver hearing aids and shows them in her palms. Behold, these are my fucks, observe how I am not giving them. This is Lana in her element: she cut her teeth on rainforest reclamation, and fire crews are nothing next to the politicos, logging companies, and cattle interests she battled in Recife. That never-ending war had cost Lana her marriage, and then she'd left Earth altogether, taking jobs developing lunar and orbital biomes for many of the same polluter corporations she'd fought for years. This is the long game, she told skeptical friends. Make it more profitable for them to chew up dead planets than to chew up our own.

Lana prowls at the edge of the pines, stalking back and forth, until the fires are doused. The smell will be in Arrigo's hair for days.

They cut home over open meadowland, then to the dirt road that leads through the fruit orchards and pollinator gardens. The sunline swelters overhead. The *Ekphrasis* is a cylinder, and greendeck is its core, rotating around an axis of artificial sun. A partial sheath around the sunline, rotating more slowly, replicates Earth's light-dark cycles. Where Arrigo, Lana, and the priest are walking, it's high noon, but on the opposite side of greendeck, it's midnight. Father Leo suggests a more westerly route, where it's late morning and less hot, but Lana has her ears in her fists.

"Look at this," Lana says. There are plums rotting on the ground beneath their trees, hairy with wasps. The entire walk, she has found neglected plants: berries unharvested, brambles unpruned. In the pollinator garden, she drops to her knees and weeds furiously, ripping out dandelions and flinging them away. Arrigo and Leo trade looks and join her. "Where are the garden teams?" she says, as if they have failed her personally. "What's going on?"

"A lot of people have been calling in sick," Arrigo says, "ever since the big party."

"Hungover?" Lana says, incredulous.

"No, I think there's a little respiratory thing going around," Father Leo offers.

Lana snorts. "Hungover."

"I think people are homesick," Arrigo says. He digs for the taproot, the soil warm on his fingers. "It makes sense, doesn't it? That rock—the sednoid, I mean, VL-something-something—that was the last piece of the Solar System we'll ever see."

Parents hang it in mobiles over cribs. It is in every schoolroom, a consensus pantheon in posters and painted foam balls. How could leaving it *not* affect people?

Lana's mouth tightens; she sighs through her nose, evaluating him. Arrigo can practically feel her condescending, like an airplane changing altitude. "It makes poetic sense," she says, and it is devastating.

Arrigo doesn't hold it against her. He knows what's at stake, what kind of pressure she's under. A closed biome needs active care or they will all die. According to Akutagawa's Law of Artificial Ecosystems— well, Arrigo doesn't recall the precise technical formulation of Akutagawa's Law, but here is the gist: An artificial ecosystem operated for maximum extraction (of food, or oxygen, or materials) will not self-sustain, but require periodic resupply to survive. On the other hand, an artificial ecosystem left to itself will not sustain, either. Dominant species will emerge, overrun the biome, and die off; and the smaller the system, the more rapidly biodiversity will collapse. Active human management is necessary to keep an artificial biome in equilibrium. Theoretically, that equilibrium could continue as long as their sunline has fuel. But no one has attempted to sustain a strictly closed biome for eighty-one years. No one has done it for eight.

Lana rises, her soiled hands shaking. Arrigo, crouched, senses a heaviness inside his chest, his belly. There's a shadow, he remembers her saying, and now he feels it, too. Like a cloud passing overhead, though the engineers haven't gotten clouds right yet. Arrigo stands, pushing off one crutch; he forgets the ship's gradient and pitches backward, falling, falling to the hard-packed earth.

THE *EKPHRASIS*'S ARTIFICIAL gravity is rotational: its spinning cylinder flings everyone centrifugally outward at 1G, even as the ship accelerates toward Luyten's Star at 0.01G. This creates a persistent one-percent grade along the ship's length—see figure 1.

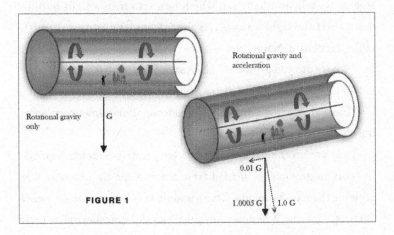

Rotational gravity and acceleration

Rotational gravity only

G

0.01 G

1.0005 G   1.0 G

FIGURE 1

It's not so terrible. Pencils roll when they fall to the floor. On greendeck, the trees grow aslant and vegetables root as if on a gentle hill. Water levels at a slight tilt in glasses and saucepans. Arrigo slips wads of paper under his chair legs and sleeps with his bed against the wall. He barely registers the grade now, not consciously. It's just that nineteen years is a long time to live tipped back. Life cranes upward, ever so slightly, toward their destination Qaf, and when he stumbles, when he loses his center and staggers, it's back to Earth. He is oriented toward Qaf—time flows there—Qaf is his eschatology, his unearthly paradise, a bizarro Eden surging with impossible life that will fill his poems with unimagined beauty.

Qaf is a note sounded along the lute string / we are the lute, he writes. He crosses it out, blowing a raspberry.

"WHY AREN'T YOU on the Vine?" Arrigo asks Mike again, on their first date. Coffee—in tin cups and saucers, at a little verdigris table. Arrigo takes Mike in, admiring his fleshiness, his thick arms and thighs, muscle and baby-fat, which he's set off in a tight button-down shirt and tight jeans. Arrigo's crutches lean against the little table, a watchful chaperone.

"Where did you grow up?" Mike says.

"Nuh-uh. Can't get out of answering, this time."

"I am answering. Did you feel safe in your hometown, coming out?"

They are on the patio of the café cooperative Sánchez Saornil-Guérin, on greendeck, shaded from the sunline by a banana tree growing through a ramada. Crows waddle between the tables, heads darting, cocking. Whenever anyone looks at them, they rattle their

pinion-feathers and pretend to peck the dirt. Arrigo and Mike's fore-
heads shine with sweat and their fingers stink of raw coffee beans.
The co-op asks members to put in an extra hour's work weekly, harvesting coffee cherries, milling, drying, and gardening. It is all very
anarcho-utopian, which seems to be Mike's thing.

Arrigo considers Mike's question. "Safe physically, sure—
emotionally, no."

Mike nods. "It wasn't safe physically, for me." He watches how
Arrigo receives this— his nostrils flare, he doesn't want sympathy.
He kicks his chair back, balancing on its rear legs. "Honestly, I've
had enough of people."

Over his head, the café's oak-beam lintel is painted with the
purple words: *EARTH IS CANCELLED*.

At the tables around them, people wear colorless hemp and home-
spun and stainless-steel rings on all their fingers. The café co-op is
the ship's dog park for heterosexuals. Well—that's unfair, as far as
numbers go it's probably no straighter a space than the labs or galleries. Still, it crackles with that anxiety Arrigo associates with a certain sort of straight people, who feel as misfit as their queer friends
but can't pour that rootlessness into an identity or ascribe it to a
specific persecution. Hence their rage, that frantic righteousness.
Mike seems to know everyone here; his attention keeps breaking to
return someone's fist bump or extremely butch nod.

Arrigo asks, "What about your parents, your friends back home,
though?"

Mike admits he used the Vine in the first month, when the data
lag was short enough to video-chat. He has a huge extended family,
so he was always on, explaining space travel to aunties or meeting
another cousin. Meanwhile, this guy he knew in high school set up a

bot that messaged him photos of giant hogs, saying, *This is the hog that fucks you today.* Every day, it was a different pig. A few days, unexpectedly, a llama.

"Jesus."

"I know, right? Some of the llamas were cute, though. I could see it."

Arrigo's parents send him photos of the small children that have befriended them since he left. Neighbors' kids, co-workers' kids, the cleaning lady's kids. Pictures of his parents playing with these alternate-reality grandkids on the front lawn; Christmas cards they've received, from progeny he has not furnished. "So basically the same thing," Mike says, grinning.

"My parents are very afraid of death," Arrigo says, "that's why they're obsessed."

His brother died when he was a baby. He was five years older than Arrigo. Arrigo never knew him but lived in his room, inherited his clothes. There were pictures of him on the dresser. Sometimes, when Arrigo's parents thought they were telling a story from Arrigo's childhood, it was actually his brother's. His parents never told him he was a replacement child, but that's what he was.

Arrigo's brother would have gone into civil engineering, like his father and grandfather. He would have built seawalls and carbon wells to rehabilitate their brutalized planet. He would have married young and at holidays, would have herded an ever-swelling flock of grandchildren over his parents' threshold.

"See? Don't you want that kind of thinking out of your head?" Mike says. He rocks on his chair legs and the ramada's shadows ripple over his face. "The weirdest thing about tattoos," he says, "is you're marking your supposed individuality with someone else's drawing. It's something someone *sold* you. And it's the same boring clichés we left behind on Earth. The Sun is hope. The phoenix is re-birth. Just stop. Do you know how many phoenixes I inked? Liter-ally, hundreds." Arrigo is scrambling to remember if he has the Sun anywhere, if he needs to come up with a good story for it. Penguin with a lawnmower, he thinks. Astrolabe. Owlfish. Climbing roses. A raccoon that looks like Cary Grant. All safely baffling. "My friend Klaus," Mike says, dropping forward decisively, with fire in his voice— and Arrigo is confused, are they still flirting, or is it just discourse from hereon out—"my friend Klaus has the right idea, he tattooed himself in corporate logos and bar codes. Because we're all fucking bought and paid for by the Foundation's investors, anyway."

"Totally," Arrigo says, totally lost.

THEY ARE ALL supposed to post on the Vine regularly—"provide content," another familiar enough phrase that deranges at a dis-tance. Arrigo tries; he follows the Foundation's guidelines. He makes it personal, but keeps it light. He describes the odd, evocative details of life on a long-haul spaceship. He talks about his projects, shares bits of research: Did you know, O people of Earth, the sednoid 2033 VL$_{115}$ has an orbit so long and eccentric, one of its years takes 13,000 of ours? But he's doing it wrong, somehow. He is guessing what peo-ple want to hear from him and at three trillion miles, his guesses misfire. He sounds like a fucking Martian. Nothing he posts gets attention, or else it gets the weird kind, trolls, bots, the desperately unhappy. *Help us*, they write, from three months in the past, *every-thing is terrible. The wild spaces are on fire. There are shootings. There are deer on the side of the highway bled to husks by ticks. 'Sup space fag go eat uranus.* Did you know, my Earth-friends, the class term "sednoid" comes from the planetesimal 90377 Sedna, named for the Inuit goddess of the underworld, the Mother of the Deep?

Christ, it feels so false and gross.

Whenever he closes the Vine app and lifts his head, groggy and eyestrained, Arrigo has the feeling of a vast, deserted parking lot and him wheeling out a shopping cart full of useless junk that has cost years off his life. Still, there is that suspicion, under the performance, a hard nub of necessity: he has something worth putting into words.

ARRIGO FINDS HIMSELF running late, again, for Melsinger's workshop. He has been on crutches two weeks but is surprised, every day, by how much of an hour he needs to cross the ship from one obligation to the next. He's been busy researching trans-Neptunian objects for M.E. Park, the deep-space philosopher, for their *Tractacus Cosmo-Philosophicus* (working title), and outer space has cost him time.

The workshop is halfway through the Act I trio when Arrigo swings in. By the wall, the great Melsinger, his idol, smashes chords out of an upright piano; in the center of the room, the singers, the dramaturg, the producer and director and others Arrigo can't place sit around an arrangement of plastic tables. In the door, he waits to feel a heat of belonging slipping around him like a bath. He waits, then finds himself a seat.

The rehearsal rooms are some of homedeck's most prosaic, dishwater spaces. Corkboard panels, acoustic drop ceiling, brown folding chairs on aquamarine carpet. Cheaply printed posters of great musicians, with photographs of Leontyne Price or Leonard Bern-stein over inspirational quotes. (When did Wagner marshal the ba-nality to declare, "Imagination creates reality"? But apparently he did.) Melsinger at the piano is a dour, badgery eminence, in a black waistcoat and round white beard, melancholy, sarcastic, with a thick, pitted nose, whose only form of exercise seems to be hunching and screaming in Lithuanian. He has decided, for his opera, to re-score the soprano's Act I aria as a duet, with the shade of the dead prima donna she replaces singing atonally under her melodic line. The music is a technical nightmare, and worse, probably genius.

Together they push through Act I, singing, reading, or humming. Where Arrigo hasn't yet supplied acceptable words, where he has, rather, supplied words Melsinger finds "unmusical," the singers use "aahs" and "oohs" or solfège syllables—*do re mi la* etc.—and Arrigo is anxious that Melsinger will leave the text like that out of spite.

Fa, fa, fa, fa fuck my life, the mezzo sings, her voice collapsing. Everyone is loopy.

Arrigo scoots his chair next to Carolyn, the first violinist. Orches-tra principals aren't supposed to attend these workshops, but union rules are malleable past the Kuiper belt. Carolyn Red Deer is the ship's chief astronomer as well; she is also Lana's girlfriend and it is his duty to befriend her. "I have a question about trans-Neptunian objects," he whispers. Melsinger and the principal winds have a shouting match over the limits of the human breath.

Carolyn answers Arrigo's questions, but there is a heaviness in her voice, deep in her chest—the area where Arrigo likewise feels heavy and sour, ever since the ship passed 2033 do-re-mi-whatever. La-na's *shadow*, again. He is certain. He should warn someone, shouldn't he?—Remy, Psychcomm—but it sounds too kooky and mysterious. Too "poetic sense." Captain, I'm sensing a great disturbance in the Force.

He is sure he is overreacting. He is sure he is talking nonsense; he always is.

"That's it! We're through," Melsinger cries, though he is laughing. Everyone is laughing and Arrigo has missed why. The composer lifts his eyes and beseeches Heaven. "I'm taking my opera to London on the first flight back!"

When we get to Qaf, will we still raise our eyes to the sky, or kiss solid, generous ground every time?

La Traviata in Space

Today I want to look at two famous pieces from Verdi's *La Traviata*, the Act I *brindisi* and Germont's aria in Act II, "Di Provenza il mar." And I want to examine them in terms of their prosody, specifically. Because the Italian language has a wonderful sound, but it's liable to fall into simple rhyme schemes and metrically regular lines, which make for predicable phrase structures in the music. We have an example of this in "Di Provenza," which is a nice enough tune, but rhythmically, it's pretty fucking dull:

Here is the context: Alfredo is a young, provincial bourgeois who has fallen in love with Violetta, a sophisticated courtesan in Paris, and convinced her to leave her benefactor and run away with him. He is doing his best to spend all his money on her, to prevent her from spending all her money on *him*; they are very much in love. His father, Germont, visits Violetta secretly to beg her to leave Alfredo, because the scandal of her—a prostitute, living unmarried with his son—threatens to derail a good marriage for Alfredo's sister. Violetta agrees and takes off. Alfredo has just read her farewell note. Germont reenters. He urges his son to forget his liaison with Violetta and return to their family home, asking: *Of Provence's sea and sun / is all memory erased?*

Now, what I want to draw your attention to is how Verdi's rhythmic setting affects the line's meter. Here, the meter is a very classical, if rarely used *ottonario doppio (tronco)*, and in *ottonario*, you'd stress the seventh syllable the most (the principal accent), and more subtly, the third syllable (the secondary accent). *Di ProVENza_il mar il **SUOL'** / chi dal COR ti cancellÒ.* There were strict rules for how composers would set those accents over the music's beat. But what Verdi and his contemporaries were finding is that those conventions produce unexciting music. They may make the music more intelligible, but at the cost of drama, vivacity. And in "Di Provenza," Verdi hits us over the head with that tradeoff. Notice how the evenly spaced rhythm all but smothers the principal and secondary accents. Try replacing each syllable with a heavy monosyllable, and you'll hear it.

Meow meow meow meow meow meow meow   meow meow meow meow meow meow meow

This is a plodding, inane rhythm, perfectly suited to the old-fashioned, stuffy values Germont embodies. Look at the rhyme scheme, and it's even worse. The verses rhyme *AB AB AB*, but the *A* and *B* lines nearly rhyme with each other—I mean, Jesus, that's a lot—but on top of that, Verdi REPEATS EVERY FUCKING LINE, inverted, so that everything rhymes internally WITH ITSELF:

> Di Provenza il mar, il suol'   chi dal cor ti cancellò?
> Chi dal cor ti cancellò   di Provenza il mar, il suol'?
> Al natio fulgente sol'   qual destino ti furò?
> Qual destino ti furò   al natio fulgente sol'?

(Meow meow meow meow meow meow meow,
quack quack quack quack quack quack quack.
Quack quack quack quack quack quack quack
meow meow meow meow meow meow meow.)

Predictability and repetition have their place, but this is hoary to the degree of parody.

Now, I want to contrast Germont's aria with the drinking song his son, Alfredo, sings in Act I, the famous brindisi, a nimble, rollicking toast to love and pleasure:

Li- bia-   mo, li- bia-mo ne' lie-   ti ca-   li- ci che la bel- lez- za in- fio-   ra

Here, the way the words sit on top of the waltz is complex, unpredictable, and lively, suited to Alfredo's exuberance and youth, and the melody is so natural and charming that, for all its metrical asymmetry, this is the number everyone leaves the opera humming.

> Let's drink from that happy cup that beauty enflowers
> and may the fleeting moment grow drunk with pleasure . . .

On the *Ekphrasis*, Dr. Malouf has me monitoring reaction wood, the "muscle" that forms in woody plants in response to stressors like gravity and wind. In a closed biome, the danger is that the lack of wind causes stalks to atrophy. The constant force of gravity isn't enough; the plant needs some irregular, unpredictable, playful stressor to stand on its own. In music, rhythm is wind in time. A gently irregular meter brings liveliness, *circulation* into Alfredo's brindisi where his father's aria is so stale and airless.

AND TO EXTRAPOLATE wildly, isn't that what queerness is to the broader human community—an asymmetry, a bit of chaos to nurse the beauty of life into its tallest flowering?

HALL Q, A new gallery installation, opens on homedeck. Arrigo is Mike's plus-one. The high, dark room houses a giant holographic projection of the planet Qaf, rotating and flickering. Look, there go its oceans, blue tinged with violet. Its continents, green with white pockmarks, which the simulation interprets as mountain snows. The colors fall on visitors' upturned faces. Arrigo finds Mike's hand in the dark. The two promises confuse, merge—the New World, and a new fever of love, *quell'amor ch'è palpito dell'universo intero*—

"Every spaceship needs a room with a big-ass hologram," Mike says, satisfied. He wired the projectors himself. He squeezes Arrigo's hand.

Qaf wobbles as the simulation updates. Streaks of gold appear on the southern continent. Pampas, Arrigo decides. Ship telescopes gather smears of spectra from red starlight glancing off the planet; from these spectra, the astrochemists determine atmospheric composition, surface colors, and other biosignatures, but since they're all layered on top of each other, it takes high-powered statistical computations to parse the data. Mike has explained it all to him, but Arrigo, virginal, is untouched by understanding.

Mike is circumspect. He squints up at the rolling ball of data and light. His mouth curls at one corner, a smile with an asterisk. He is thinking about Earth, Arrigo supposes. Thinking: Fine, fine, anywhere but home.

At the end of the night, as they walk and limp back to Arrigo's quarters, he asks Mike about his childhood, and Mike answers so vaguely, Arrigo can't remember what he actually said. But that night, he will dream of Mike as Dorothy Gale, a little brown girl in pigtails and blue gingham being pelted by trees throwing their apples. *Suck it, homo*, the trees catcall.

At his door, Arrigo thinks, I'm going to take this one slow. He kisses Mike chastely and does not invite him in. Mike lingers outside the door, brow creasing—Arrigo watches through a peephole. Mike looks up. He mouths a question, suddenly, as if to a bird flying past him.

HERE IS THE story of the frog tattoo on Mike's arm, which he will not tell Arrigo for a few years more. Mike grew up in New Eden, Arizona, a recent piece of Tucson sprawl already on the decline—a lush, lawned suburb planted with maple and flowering dogwood and rapidly running out of water, its white evangelical population giving way to Mexican immigrant families and a tiny Filipino enclave, itself constantly mistaken for Mexican. At school, the white kids picked on Mike for being brown and the brown kids picked on him for being lumped in with them. His teachers quickly pegged him for a "sensitive" boy, an innuendo his parents completely failed to grasp. In his fourth-grade classroom was a terrarium, and in the terrarium was a canyon tree frog slowly dying of despair. Canyon tree frogs are delicate, adapted for a highly specific ecology. They have suckers on their palms, bands on their legs, and beautiful spots all over. They live in the crevices between rocks by healthy desert streams. The terrarium had nothing suitable for such a creature. But the kids blamed Mike for the frog's wasting away, because the frog was his classroom chore and because they knew, on an unconscious level, the adults wanted him blamed. When the frog died, someone nailed it to the underside of his desk.

Mike's extended family—the elaborate network of uncles, godparents, and quasi-relatives that mediates a Pinoy life with the rest of the universe—couldn't protect him from New Eden's cruelty. Unequal to the sheer intricacy of American racism, embarrassed by homophobia, tangled in constructs of sin, debt, and manliness, they said all the wrong things, offered totally maladapted solutions. It was a system built for another world—a home that soured more and more in Mike's imagination. According to diaspora time, these are the years when Mike is supposed to wonder where he came from. To feel at sea in crowds of white, sunburnt faces, to make vague plans to visit his parents' home province and meet his distant cousins, to learn his mother's recipes for lumpia, to buckle down and learn Tagalog for real, this time. But that clock is so irreparably fucked and Mike can never visit his parents' home province. His bitterness smooths over the guilt. He feels sorry for the Pinoys on the ship who haven't had the *utang na loob* beaten out of them. He sees them at Mass on

Sundays, reciting a Passion strange to him. They spend hours doom-scrolling the Vine, watching their old barangays get chewed up by typhoons and swallowed by rising seas.

TIME CATCHES, ONE morning.

Across the ship, people wake afraid. They are beyond the last solid rock, beyond rescue, in a bottle speeding through infinite night. Lana and Carolyn wake with twin headaches. Arrigo, in his quarters, throws off his quilts in a panic. "Lights!" he shouts, but the room doesn't answer; it's only a room. On the other side of homedeck, Mike Faustino feels neither pain nor panic, just an ungodly exhaustion that holds him flat to his bed for hours.

Throughout the ship, crew members report the same experiences: lethargy, dread, restlessness, a sense of running up against a wall. When did it start? That morning—or the night before. Or the night of the party, weeks ago: Mike felt tired and bitter, so he didn't go. The party for the sednoid, 2033 VL$_{115}$, Mother of the Deep, goddess of the underworld, tiny, fiery rose in the black. Nearly five years out and they're still passing things bound to the Sun. But it'll be *twenty* years before they're truly outside the Solar System, Carolyn told Arrigo. Everything within two light-years orbits the Sun, more or less.

Arrigo has found multiple versions of the goddess Sedna's legend in the ship's libraries, but they all end with her thrown into the sea by her father. When she clings to the side of his kayak, he chops off her fingers, which sink and become the monsters of the deep, whales, seals, walruses. The reason for her father's violence varies. In one story, she is a giant whose terrible hunger stirs her to attack her parents. In another, she is a maiden who spurns the suitors her father has chosen for her and marries a dog. These stories are closer in meaning than they seem. There is the common offense of dissatisfaction, the reckless desire for more or other than what our families offer us.

Look where it's brought us, Arrigo thinks. Exiles still in sight of the city towers.

Here is what Arrigo knows, as he scrambles for a light switch: that he has made a terrible mistake leaving Earth. The expedition will fail and everyone on Earth will scorn them for their presumption, bunch of sissies fumbling the starshot. What if Mike is wrong, and when you leave behind everything you know, all the received forms, clichés, and oppressive constructs, you get only noise? This shriveled, methane-choked sednoid, this insane crone of a world, is all they can hope to encounter in the long void between stars. Can anyone survive an eighty-year night on so remote a promise as Qaf?

Could you?

Here is what Lana knows, as she climbs the stairs to greendeck, breathless: that she is a botched person. She couldn't do shit for the Earth and in running away from her failure, she's only found more. This biome will collapse—today, tomorrow, it doesn't make a difference. Everything will die and it is still her fault. She isn't made to pull it off. Too weak, too slow, too deaf, too broken, too ugly, too charmless, even dogs don't like her, even plants and tubers think she's sort of a bitch. She tries to chop a gnarled yam for her dinner and the knife breaks in her hand. It is irreplaceable.

Here is what Mike knows, as he pulls the blankets over his head: that he's a fool, that he's damaged goods and everyone senses it. Arrigo hasn't called him, not since closing his door in Mike's face. He's figured Mike out, seen through the smile and muscle all the way to his rotten core. All the bulk he's put on, the no-bullshit engineering brain he's hardwired, the aggressive radicalism he's holed up in, none of it can hide the soft kid getting his heart broken by yet another awkward white boy.

Years ago, on his first construction shift on the *Ekphrasis*, when the space elevator had cleared the atmosphere and he saw Earth dropping away powerlessly—and the relief hit him, and he knew he'd apply for the expedition—for a moment, he'd thought he might belong somewhere. Now he curls into a ball under the quilts. He belongs at the bottom of the ocean.

Lana hauls Arrigo up to greendeck, crutches and all. Bring as many people as you can to the savannah zone, she tells him.

On greendeck, Arrigo's head clears a little. Perception brightens again, as if the shadow of a cloud has passed. Four hundred expedition members have skipped their work shifts, calling in sick or lying in bed, despondent, but Lana has collected a small posse. Carolyn kneels, face in the bushes. Father Leo is there, with Mike Faustino and others in his little parish. Arrigo does a double take but is too distracted to think much about Mike's contradictions. They stand in the withered scrub, confused and stricken and hot. Mike waves listlessly to Arrigo and Arrigo forgets to respond.

Lana passes out watering cans, hand rakes, and Bermuda grass seed. "Cover as much ground as you can," she says, struggling to articulate. "It's grass, grass, grass. Got it?"

They activate the grassland, then the fog desert. Fast-growing Bermuda grass will suck carbon dioxide out of the biome and exhale oxygen; meanwhile, emergency oxygen candles are being distributed. Arrigo isn't completely following, even after Lana explains. "Hypoxia? That's what's making everyone lose it?"

"The brain's extremely sensitive even to small oxygen differentials," Lana says. "That's why cities at elevation have higher suicide rates. Why everyone in Denver's so goddamn miserable, for example."

Lana's ex-wife lives in Denver, Arrigo recalls.

"Are you sure it's just that?" he says. "It feels like some kind of mass existential crisis."

She is patient. "Look, I've seen the numbers. Oxygen levels are down, CO_2 is up. It's that simple. It's those fires last week—I told them, remember? Too much carbon."

Arrigo isn't satisfied, but he keeps his mouth shut. He refills his seed bag and limps out over the scrub. He can go without crutches for short walks, now, though the boot is cumbersome and itches in the heat. Here the sunline's glare is hideous. There's no sky, no blue, nothing but grass and chaparral curving up in walls of gold-brown until they climb into night-side. Father Leo catches up to Arrigo. "You notice it too, don't you," Leo says in a low voice, though there is no one in earshot.

"Me?" says Arrigo.

Leo raises a finger stuck with grass seed. "That *wrongness*—isn't it a little too familiar?"

For here is what Leo knows: that he has wrestled this shadow before, in a prior dark night of the soul. It's the same shadow cast by those who never saw or refused to see Leo as he was; who would strike that gift of him from his outstretched hand. A long shadow, one he had hoped might not reach so far to follow them. Outer space, he'd hoped, would be like the desert to the Church Fathers, an openness where the flesh's interfering veils stretch thin. He doesn't hear his Creator any better in this emptiness, though. It's as if God has a different voice in space, a colder, stygian, submolecular timbre, a mathematical murmuration. When Father Leo prays, he no longer hears that steadying voice he associates with the Holy Spirit—just the soft gibberish of quantum flux.

ARRIGO AND THE priest have met from time to time at M.E. Park's breakfast table, Arrigo delivering his research notes, Father Leo there to urge God into M.E.'s deep-space ontologies. Vaguely, M.E. wants them to get along, but Arrigo regards Father Leo as something of a chump with a martyr complex, and Leo looks back at Arrigo with that aloof, indicting gaze of a double in a mirror.

He remembers when Father Leo came out. Cable news fed for a week on the footage: at a major interfaith climate protest in Chicago, at a podium in front of thousands, a charismatic young priest proclaiming *He created me trans and blessed me*. Splashy, Arrigo conceded, but he didn't trust it. Priests are supposed to be a finger pointing to God; when they declare *This is my body*, it's a more supernatural transubstantiation they're asserting. Though, to be fair to the priest, Leo *was* trying to say something like that. Something like, just as he possessed a nature higher and truer than his childhood sex characteristics, there is a God that sits above mere biology. That, to truly thrive, Creation needs us to see not only ice shelves breaking into the sea but the living Spirit inside them; not only trees but dryads. The nature above Nature.

Arrigo will give him this: Leo has made every cardinal in Rome miserable.

M.E.'s thinking has traveled the same cut from gender to metaphysics, over the course of their longer career. They've arrived, a little worse for wear, at process philosophy. All reality is unfolding processes, interrelated and interdynamic. Gender and sexuality are dynamic, too, not truths or qualities, still less aspects of the soul, but modes of relationship between the individual and every other real process in existence. The unfolding process that is Arrigo, or more precisely, the society of successive Arrigos that concresce across time, *is* not male and *is* not gay; rather, he *males* and *gays* the universe. His lovers and friends, his toothbrush, his boots, passing comets, all are *gayed* by him and *gay* him back. And while this *gaying* may continue stably, it is never immutable. Every process affects every other. Every face in the crowd acts on Arrigo's *maling* and *gaying*, however microscopically—and his *whiting* and *neurotypicalling* and *poeting*, too. And on and on. No man-ness is an island.

The process that is Arrigo and the process that is Leo, sitting across the process that is M.E.'s hashbrowns, do not relish the idea that they will leave M.E.'s rooms having dented each other's genders. "Tough tits," the process that is M.E. says—says to all the universe becoming.

MOODS LIFT ACROSS the ship. Boosted oxygen mellows tempers, comforts the afflicted, wakes the dead. Crew members report feeling years younger; they run up and down homedeck's corridors for the zest of it. In a week, the savannah zone ripples in its dark green coat, and the desert has bloomed. Arrigo and Lana comb greendeck together, patching biorhythms that have fallen out of step. Mostly, an obscene amount of weeding and pruning. They rake the scum off standing water and uproot bamboo culms. Arrigo is out of his walking boot and misses it. His ankle feels tender, unsupported. He worries he'll roll it again and picks over the uneven ground, scanning for gopher holes (did they *bring* gophers?) while Lana worries over the horses. They are inessential to the biome, but people love them, *she* loves them, and they are not doing well. They hardly eat, but only drag their teeth along the ground, black lips curled, swinging their heads from side to side.

Moods are lifted, Arrigo breathes normally, but still he feels like crap inside. He doesn't have the heart to tell Lana this. He wants things to be how they were. When they hug at the end of the shift, he slackens in her arms, like he could fall asleep there, a dopey, malnourished koala bear hanging from her eucalyptus shoulders.

In Hall Q, he sits gaping at Qaf's hologram and tries writing. If I could put a song in that planet, he thinks.

Other artists pull up chairs with the same notion, scribbling, sketching, colonizing the planet with their queer imaginations. Arrigo feels so remote from them. Daring and subversion come so naturally to these others, but not to him. The antagonism, the prurience, the camp, the war cry of high faggotry: when he tries it himself, the results are grisly, a bad impression. Maybe he isn't queer at all; maybe he is just a cocksucker.

The tables in homedeck's endless corridors are secondhand hotel furniture. They hold red plastic Ganeshas and Mississippi riverboats modeled from hammered brass and commemorative porcelain plates painted with rosy-cheeked Dutch children.

The ship throws another party in the oculus ballroom. Everyone is determined to recapture their spirit of adventure, to drown heartsorrow in sensation and surprise. Arrigo and Lana trip on her genius mushrooms, *Psilocybe mexicana*. The ballroom is so crowded no one can move. Bodies envelop one another, their heat and mass and salty ripeness. They strobe, they flicker, they bear each other up on their jostling elbows, a membrane of hips and elbows, cherry petals on water. Reality and time drain funneling into Arrigo's vision. Euphoria jellies his bones and singes his nerve-ends. It devastates him; he is still so raw from his loathing. His body clutches Lana's. She is his trellis. Her eyes in the strobe-bursts show the backs of her own cosmogenic visions like the reverse of a tapestry. His ankle is still sore, still angry with his choices. Lana hooks a hand under the leg and cocks it against her and he arches his back, and a tremendous music rises inside him, dissonance aching for resolution, but only rising and rising, speeding further away from its home key.

Arrigo has no memory of dancing. He thinks they must be standing as still as posts on the floor of rolling stars. Then they are standing inside his quarters. His eyes are closed, the planet Qaf is behind his lids like a tree as big as a mountain, its canopy flowering with every known blossom and a hundred million unknown. It is dark. It is light. Arrigo, in front of his bedroom closet, inspects the floor-to-ceiling stack of spiral notebooks he's brought, because how much paper is eighty years' worth, anyway?

"Foresight's overrated," Lana says. She sways like a tree. "Planning is good, but on a voyage this long, nothing can be planned out so far." She turns to him. "Adaptation, resourcefulness: that's survival."

Yes, he thinks. Or says, desperately. In any event: yes.

He is inside her, under her, her warm cunt slips around his penis so smoothly he thinks he'll cry. The anatomy shames him, it is so soft, so suitable. This is where his cock is supposed to go, he thinks, I'm all wrong and backwards. Lana's mouth sucks at his; her teeth scrape his lip, she yanks his hair so she can kiss at his throat. Look at me, she demands. She cups his cheek; her fingers smell like mushrooms. Look at me. He groans, bucks into her. His asshole buttons as he thrusts up, as though some universe-spirit is in bed with them with its claws at his ribcage fucking him into her. When he comes, he's like a burnt matchhead. Lana grinds on him, breasts rocking with her force. She slaps him, not hard, just enough to focus him on her—if he forgets to focus, his mind rolls out of his head on to the floor.

Watching Lana wipe down, after, he thinks, I'm a fucking disaster. He is not sober and feeling sick and fearful about it. In the bathroom light, Lana's naked back explains the glimpses of ink he's seen around her collar. Her shoulders down to her sacrum hold a manticore, a lion with the face of a woman, a scorpion tail, and dragon wings. Its mane curls up the back of Lana's neck and its stinger folds over her trapezius like a scarf. It's already lost a tuft of fur from its center as the vitacene ink breaks down, refilling her with life. Lana glances back over her shoulder. A complicated, uncertain look. The manticore winks at him.

"That's Ethel," she says, and wrings the cloth tight.

When she is gone, he takes his whore's bath and wraps himself in his quilts, wondering if he will be normal in the morning.

HERE IS THE story of the manticore tattoo on Lana's back, which Lana doesn't remember drunkenly confessing to Arrigo, and Arrigo doesn't remember drunkenly hearing. Lana's wedding day was perfect—or at least, irreproachable. She wore a custom tux and Johanna wore a white satin dress in a mermaid cut with a tulle veil. The cake was white and vegan; so were most of the guests, Lana joked. This was Boulder, Colorado. It was June. The wedding arch was myrtle, blush roses, and hydrangeas. Jo had four bridesmaids and Lana, four groomsmen. Lana found herself chatting up one of Jo's bridesmaids later at the reception. She had no intention of sleeping with her, not at her own wedding, what do you take her for. But she was aware that she *could*. Jo's friend was reading a fantasy novel with a manticore on its cover, which had caught Lana's eye. The bridesmaid said it was the most misogynist book she'd ever read; she said she wanted to know her enemy. Lana looked over her shoulder at Johanna dressed as a wedding-mermaid and felt a conviction wash over her that her marriage was doomed.

Officially, Lana's work schedule was what wrecked them. But that's true only in a narrowly cropped sense. Lana's work schedule meant she was gone for months at a time, which made monogamy a tall order. That and the absolute bounty of Brazilian lesbians that flowed, by some secret law, to rainforest reclamation projects. Lana's work schedule meant she couldn't be serious about wanting a baby, according to Johanna, even though Lana said she was and even though it was obvious (to anyone that *knew* her) that she would fall utterly in love with any new, helpless life fighting into being, even the dippiest sprout grown in a crack in the sidewalk, even if she was that sidewalk. Lana dreamed one night of Jo leading a manticore on a fine silver chain and the next day, they broke up.

The name? Ethel was Jo's grandmother; it's what they'd planned to name their daughter.

THE NEXT MORNING is no better for Arrigo, and he carries his air of disaster into the workshop for Melsinger's opera. His muscles are drowsy; he feels stupid, soiled, like a schoolkid sitting in his urine.

He's given Lana too much sway over him. He is late showing up to his own decisions. He sees himself doing it, but he can't stop. Miserably, he tracks the slide of Carolyn's elbow as she bows her violin, the regulation of her shoulders and the discipline of her torso under Melsinger's dark, flaring attention, *for here there is no place that does not see you.*

You must change your life.

"I can't sing this," the mezzo-soprano tells the room. Shakes her head. "It's unsingable."

She collects the sheet music from her stand, searches the long tables arranged horseshoe around her, and delivers Arrigo the stack. Folding chairs give up metal groans as bodies pivot to face the librettist. The music is no problem. They've run it with solfège syllables a dozen times. It's the words that don't work. It's Arrigo holding them up.

"Back to do-re-mi," Melsinger tells the mezzo. He turns to Arrigo, monstrously patient. "I'm going to recommend some books on writing for voice."

Arrigo wants to crawl under the table and die but manages only the first part. The thing is, he's probably already read whatever books Melsinger has in mind. He knows his metrical theory; he's fluent in the forms. He's done the work. But he doesn't sing, so he hasn't internalized the failure of sounds, how a word like '*him*' dies on a high note and '*help*' mangles a vocal line.

The plastic tables come donated from some decommissioned school lunch hall. Arrigo's fingertip traces prehistoric initials on their undersides, cretaceous dried gum. From here, he can see Mike Faus-

tino sitting in the back of the rehearsal room, his broad body stress-
less in his chair, all charm and solidity. Mike ducks to one side and
smiles at him beneath the table. Arrigo's heart breaks with relief.

Together they climb to greendeck, cut through soybean fields,
and get themselves lost in the cedar forest. The cedars are adoles-
cents, barely twice Arrigo's height, so the shade is sparse and the
forest floor busy with understory—sedge, honeysuckle, fir and hem-
lock saplings, Virginia creeper. When Arrigo's ankle aches, they stop
and he leans on Mike's shoulder, with Mike's arm warm around his
waist. A screech owl watches camouflaged against a cedar's trunk,
two molten gold eyes in the cracked bark.

"It's all a fiasco until it isn't," Arrigo says, to himself as much as
anyone.

"Don't let them push you around," Mike says. "Do you believe in
what you've written? Nothing's *unsingable*, that's nonsense."

Arrigo isn't so sure he does believe in what he's written. Honestly, he figured Melsinger would rewrite most of it anyway—he has
a reputation—and he, Arrigo, just needed to land close enough to the
mark. Mike's features sharpen as he argues; the line of his cheeks
seems to hone, as if objection makes him more precisely himself.
Half of Arrigo's brain is busy revising, fitting Act III dialogue into
eleven-syllable lines and the composer's byzantine melodic structures. The other half is still despairing over Lana, how supple and
raw to her he's become.

Arrigo hungers for form, rubric.

They come to a patch of wild nasturtiums, rich satiny orange
over green. Arrigo picks a flower and offers it to Mike. Mike threads
it through the buttonhole of his ratty red polo, at the bottom of the
V-neck, where a curl of chest ink sneaks into view.

DURANTE: It's like that moment, in *La Traviata*: Violetta gives
Alfredo a flower, telling him to come see her when it's wilted,
and he does some quick math and then he's all like— "*O ciel!*
Tomorrow!" The flower is measuring time according to life,
not life according to time.

FAUSTINO: *(wincing)*
Mm. Shoot. Listen—

DURANTE: Wh-what's the matter?

Mike unfastens the nasturtium and hands it back to Arrigo, who
watches dizzily. In training, they told everyone not to turn their heads
too quickly or they'd feel a Coriolis effect in their inner ears, due to
the rotation—that's what Arrigo feels now, but in an organ far more
interior.

"We're not in an opera," Mike says. "This is *my* story. Or it's ours,
at least."

Arrigo eats the nasturtium. It's a sweet, then peppery, radish
taste. It clears his nose.

"Look, I like you. OK? I like that you love that stuff you vinecast
about. That's all fine. But I'm not your Alfredo. I'm me. And I need
you to see *me*, or this isn't even worth trying."

'*Me*' is another one of those unsingable words, Arrigo thinks.
Try it. Belt it in your upper register. The note won't speak.

La Traviata in Space

If you've heard one piece from *La Traviata*, it's Alfredo's brindisi,
which we looked at in the last vinecast. But if you've heard two, the
second is "Sempre libera," Violetta's big Act I cabaletta, which we'll
discuss today. And I want to make the opposite claim this time: that

for all his formal innovation, Verdi has written an aria intelligible *only* in the context of its conventions.

If you've heard the piece performed alone, or seen a clip, you could be forgiven for taking "Sempre libera" as Violetta's exuberant affirmation of her life of pleasures, *I must run madly from joy to joy,* etc. The music is ingratiating, her voice is at its most powerful, and the libretto seems straightforward: Alfredo has offered her love, and although charmed by the idea, she decides this is "folly" and embraces her freedom. *I want to live my life in the paths of pleasure,* she says. Why not take her at her word?

And that's not totally wrong, but it is incomplete.

Verdi and his audiences' experience of "Sempre libera" would have been structured according to several conventions that nowadays seem remote. First, it's part of a traditional "double aria," consisting of a slow, lyrical, contemplative song (the *cavatina*) followed by a fast piece that re-engages with the plot (the *cabaletta*). "Sempre libera" forms a dramatic unit with the *cavatina* "Ah, fors'è lui," in which Violetta considers Alfredo's offer with genuine longing. The "forever free" bit is only half the story.

Second, Verdi's audience would have been well-versed in a different stock form—the mad scene. A favorite in *bel canto*, the mad scene features the heroine soprano, pushed to extremes by intense disappointment, escaping into a delirium as she fantasizes a happier reality. The mad scene's formal characteristics—*coloratura* flourishes that derange the structured melodies; dance rhythms that break off; abrupt shifts in dynamics and tempo; even the intrusion of other voices (usually the men singing something like, "Oh pity! She's nuts!")—all of these appear or are subtly echoed in "Sempre libera." Violetta isn't literally mad, she isn't unraveling like Lucia or Ana or

Elvira, but these formal echoes suggest Violetta's exhilaration for fleeting pleasures is a kind of fantasy she escapes into whenever the burden of her fatal disease overwhelms her. And that works only because Verdi can expertly deploy the *bel canto* conventions he's moving away from.

Kids need structure, right? It's not the worst thing to grow up with a framework that mediates and organizes the world around you. If we break from those structures later, it's only when the world has been made sufficiently intelligible for us to move on; its freedom comes to us late enough to see it as a choice, rather than chaos and emptiness.

Verdi chafed against the Italian language's metric regularity, but it was the language he articulated his restlessness in. Those hoary formal conventions of *cavatina* and *cabaletta* and mad scene were how he created dramatic meaning. And this ship is a structure. When I get stir-crazy, when the ceilings feel too low or the lack of sky and real sunlight or fresh air make me feel trapped in a bottle, I go to the oculus ballroom and look at the dead irradiated vacuum of space between my feet. I remember I'm alive *because* I'm in a rigid structure, and not out there, in a freedom as vast and complete as death itself.

IN THE MANGROVE habitat, Arrigo floats his toes out of the brackwater, his pelvis curled, his arms hooked over knobby, amphibious roots. The day is almost ending, but there are no sunsets here, no ardent horizons, only the sunline's sheath edging over the white glare. It's been five years since he last experienced the generosity of a sunset. Up and to the right, the rainforest zone is spending its midday in cloud. The biome engineers are beta-testing a storm made of fog and it swells and falls like a massive fluttering tapestry.

Arrigo should be working, making something of his time, doing *any*thing—even bathing, but in this mucky, sulfurous water, he is only getting dirtier. Lana said it was good for the skin, but maybe she just wanted to see if he'd fall for it. He savors this brief thrill of bitterness. She is avoiding him, too, ever since they had sex. Arrigo inhales foul air until his stomach squirms. His libretto is a failure. His poetry is a joke. Mike's going to give up on him sooner or later. He needs to learn how to not lean on these things so hard, how to stand on his own two feet—but not here and not now, because the ground is muck, stones, and the mussel shells that live on stones. If he were to attempt it, he'd only slice up his toes.

Balanced on a mangrove root is a razor blade—patient, available, neutral. During the hypoxia episode, two crew members tried to kill themselves. M.E., who sits on Psychcomm, told Arrigo about the attempts. M.E. was disturbed, but Arrigo thinks he understands the temptation, at least in the abstract. Suicide as an attempt to wrestle the mind-breaking vulnerability of deep-space travel into an illusion of control, etc. Arrigo doesn't want to die; he just wants to go mad. A spell of madness, like a vacation from reality. No responsibility, no failure, no blame, no rejection. There has to be a padded room somewhere on the ship, in those empty stretches of homedeck, where Arrigo can dance around in a gauzy slip flinging flowers and make believe he's marrying the king or some shit.

The vapors hanging over the mangrove swamp are so thick and wet and smelly, it's like the air could grow mushrooms. It smells like day-old Easter lilies here, like sulfur and salt, like the Earth's volcanic cunt, like life itself in its messiest, tentative gestation.

"Mind if I join you?"

Arrigo looks up with a jolt. The priest, Leo, is already stripping down to his briefs. Arrigo, frozen, watches as Leo splashes into the silty water.

"Your hair," Leo says admiringly. "Oh, wow."

Leo is about ten years older than him, smiling, energetic and small, though not thin, with a trim brown beard squaring his face. His body is inscribed in vitacene marginalia like a medieval codex, hares with broadswords riding snails over his collarbone, devils dragging St. Anthony up and down his ribs; on his arms, angels; on his back, the Tree of Life. Arrigo catches himself scrutinizing Leo's chest for double-incision scars. Leo catches him, too, and his smile fades.

"I'm sorry," Arrigo says. His eyes roll away in a panic to the bank, the orchids, the sawgrass singing with bullfrogs. "I didn't mean to—"

"You people are obsessed." Leo sinks until he is only a head sitting on top of the brown brackwater. "It's creepy."

Leo sighs, but his expression quickly softens. He is not an angry Father, just disappointed.

"In Rome, you know," the priest says, "one of the grounds put forward for declaring my ordination illicit is that I've mutilated myself. They consider me a woman, which is enough, but because I was baptized male, they're shoring up their case. No one who's voluntarily mutilated himself can be a priest. That goes all the way back to the fourth century, to the First Council of Nicea. There was a problem with overzealous priests castrating themselves. *Making themselves eunuchs for the kingdom of Heaven's sake*, as Jesus says. Origen was accused of it, although he says, in his Gospel commentaries, that only a fool would take Christ's words there literally. Takes one to know one, maybe."

"I'm really sorry," Arrigo says.

"Forgive me, but you are and you aren't. I know that look. I'm the ugly stepsister who's chopped off her heel to fit her foot into the glass slipper, right? Something like that? Tell me if I'm being unfair."

Arrigo says nothing. He frowns and floats his feet to the surface. Father Leo provokes him to self-scrutinize in a way M.E. and other trans folk don't. Gender as performative, as fluid, never bothered him. He relates, the idea even affirms him in his femme-ier moments. But Leo, his mind always on souls, casts his maleness as an interior reality so powerful, it resists everything outside it, even the body, whereas Arrigo has done exactly the opposite, has lopped off parts of himself for the love and approval of other people. He's sanded down his edges, squeezed into his brother's hand-me-downs. Even Arrigo's tattoos are evasions—ironic, mystifying, kidding. Chimeras and conversation pieces, things to talk about without showing himself.

"What the fuck are we, Leo?" he asks. "Are we even human? Did God make a mistake?"

"A mistake?" The question amuses Leo, or he's pretending it does.

"Yeah. Putting your soul in the wrong body. Making my parts want to go in unproductive places."

"That's not how I'd describe dysphoria. Is that really what you think gayness is?"

"You know what I'm getting at. We came out mixed up, upside-down."

Leo sweeps his arms through the water, making muck angels; the waves roll and knock into Arrigo's chest. "You know, Origen had a terrific theory for mistakes in the Gospels. Well—don't call them *mistakes*. Inconsistencies. Chronologies that don't line up square. He said God planted those defects as stumbling-blocks for literalists, so we couldn't take these texts as mere histories, but had to look for a deeper, spiritual truth within them. It's like an inoculation against fundamentalism. Maybe, if we are aberrations, we're still not accidents. We're stumbling-blocks for gender fundamentalists." Leo squints, cocks an eyebrow. "But you don't believe in God."

"Oh? Does it show?" Arrigo says. He grapples and hoists himself up the tangle of roots with his elbows. Around them, bullfrogs belching in close harmony.

"Let's talk about nature, then," Leo says. "God is merciful, but Creation definitely isn't. If something doesn't work, it dies out. If a species or a trait isn't functioning exceptionally well, it gets pushed out by something that is—like these dang bullfrogs, good Lord. What I'm saying is, nature doesn't keep anything around out of fondness or pity, but gender-nonconforming people and same-sex attraction have been around—forever, I think? As far back as we can look and in every culture. We don't propagate the trait sexually. So how are we here?"

"We have very sad straight sex," Arrigo says. "We have an indirect reproductive advantage—we're the helpers in the nest, we enhance the prospects of our nieces and nephews passing on our genes, something like that. It's . . . I don't know, I don't know genetics. What were you going to say?"

Father Leo is somehow smug and sheepish at once. "I don't know, Arrigo. I don't need to have a purely materialist explanation—I've got trans souls and God's mysterious plans to work with. I don't know how you square that circle without them."

Arrigo scrabbles upright out of the water and sits in the nest of roots. He's dressed only in swamp, but is too indignant to be embarrassed. "What? Are you serious? I thought you were setting me up for some sort of brilliant evangelization. Aren't you trying to convert me?"

"Oh, how pompous." Leo is positively gleeful to disappoint him.

"Whatever. I've got to get back to work." Arrigo clambers and sloshes back to the bank. He has his hyacinths in the greenhouse to check on. He towels off with his back turned.

"Don't forget this."

Arrigo turns and the priest is holding out his razor blade. Arrigo's heart sinks. He takes it and snaps it into a case he has in the pocket of his jeans. "Look, so we're clear—"

"I won't tell anyone."

"It's not like I'm suicidal."

"No. I understand. You just wanted the option."

Arrigo lingers. "I don't want you to leave here thinking you saved my life or anything," Arrigo says. "Because you didn't."

Leo holds up his hands. "Wouldn't dream of it."

"Good. Because I've got hyacinths." Arrigo frowns again; he almost explains himself, but better to leave it at that. End on a baroque note. He dresses and leaves the priest in the water.

The truth is, he does feel better, and part of it *is* the hyacinths. Hyacinths' purple is one of the greatest colors on Earth, painfully voluptuous, saturated with depth and texture, the purple of love potions in farces. He knows Lana, if asked, would explain why the color is reproductively useful or how flowers sustain the biome's pollinator community and all that, but he luxuriates in their rude excess of beauty, their pointless, unthinking exuberance. In answer to the absurd fragility of life, here is an equally absurd surplus.

The rainforest's midday fogstorm has spread down into greendeck's afternoon and evening longitudes. It's a funny storm, not the high, black thunderheads that put hard-to-please gods into people's minds, but a ground cloud, churning and billowing as it walks, growing top-heavy and falling again as rain. Fat droplets thud into the soil along Arrigo's path. A wooly, blue mist draws over the sunline. The rain pools and ravels the earth and spills down the ramps and stairways that lead to homedeck. Hyacinths, nasturtiums, cornflowers, and peonies, Arrigo thinks. Gardens helplessly retching color in a jury-rigged extrasolar spring, a million buds flourishing in deep night. Tendrils straining into open space, with no purpose but extension.

Earth's gaudy gratuity swelling into the stars.

||||||

ACT TWO

You, who are so good, so just and so kind-hearted, must not let yourself be influenced, must not absorb the ideas of a community which—it really needs to be said—at one time did not even consider me worthy to be its church organist.
—Letter of Giuseppe Verdi to Antonio Barezzi, 21 Jan. 1852

The engines cut at nineteen years. The one-percent grade they have climbed for two decades, one morning, is level. A week of stumbling ensues. Martial Melsinger, who uses a wheelchair now, and M.E. Park, who always has, try not to gloat at the people flailing around on two feet. As the grade falls off, so does that sense of physically anticipating the planet Qaf. As if the ship is saying to them, *This alone is your life*—the long, long now—*not what's to come.*

In the empty oculus ballroom, Arrigo and Mike make love against the portal. Stars roll beneath them, everywhere; they float radically free, cosmically unmoored. They grip each other with their legs, squirming into conjunction, giddy with infinity, lost in and on all fours before the great nothingness suspending them. The vertigo of it makes their contact delirious and overhot, hairs on end, organs swinging arrogant, but the cold of space seeps through and chills their flesh: a breath of ice on bare shins.

In bed, in their shared quarters, Arrigo runs the tip of a finger over his lover's acne, a vitacene side effect Mike can't seem to shake. Suspicion darts from Mike's eyes, then self- apology, then both fall away and leave the shy, floundering wonder that one's misfit body could be a place of adoration to another. Is this what perpetual youth is? Arrigo thinks. They are in their forties but young men. Not just in their bodies, but spiritually, too. The years flutter by like paper. Is this the future, this eruption, life boiling over the rim of the Earth into the bigger universe?

Arrigo's heart is a hearth. Glowing, sustained.

When he's giving Mike head, he thinks: Poetry is like blowing humankind. Arrigo is not an engineer, he does not make useful things like Lana's biomes or Mike's circuits, but he brings free and unproductive pleasure to those who do. He loves the rhythm of his work, its spit-slick, its sound, like a tide slopping in a canal, the movement of a whole ancient ocean collected into a bobbing slurp, lifting and falling, rhyming, returning.

Martha Graham: *When I was making the dance called "Ekstasis" in 1933, I discovered, for myself, the relationship between the hip and the shoulder.* Arrigo's mouth works Mike into similar discoveries and collects revelation on the tongue.

The art the expedition members make grows remote from Earth. Inaccessible by Vine transmission, digitally ineffable. Gallery installations full of perfumes and trick angles. Works bound up in the scale of spacetime: twenty-hour concert overtures based on cosmic background radiation and high-resolution films of unchanging void. And weather! Biocomm turns its storms over to the artists to introduce unpredictability and character into the rains. No one understands the weather artists' vision or rule or how exactly, as their manifesto declares, they *imitate and confront, through heat, liquid, and time, the interdependency of artifice and nature*; but everyone is pleased to be baffled. The best art has an echo of divine mystery to it, a sense of participating in an experience beyond ourselves with its own, illegible intention.

Land art makes a wicked comeback on the ship with no spare land. In *The Garden of Unearthly Delights*, the Argentine landscape painter, Tello, grows an orchard of inedible fruit, onyx-fleshed tangerines and figs seeded with artificial diamonds. The trans sculptress Jayne Fielding weaves a giant, living bird's nest out of blackberry bramble, willow, yarrow, and sage. (Title: *Becoming Illusion No. 4*.) Typical, that artists should want to work with the scarcest, most important resource—here, arable soil—as if art itself is a response to scarcity, an insistence that beauty is as necessary as food.

The same perverse and rebel impulse animates Arrigo and Mike's sex, they refuse to contain what Earth has taught them to keep private. They map the ship with their fucking. They rut like hares in the woods, in service tunnels, even in Qaf itself—inside the planetary hologram, in the ozone-smelling fog that suspends the projection, Arrigo devours the planet of Mike's ass. They are in love. Mike, who so mistrusts entanglements, who keeps one foot lifted to hop off the rug before it's pulled out from under him, is intimate only reck-lessly, vulnerable only completely. Arrigo sees Mike's full-heartedness and answers with his own. It's their love song. The two men hear their selves swelling out toward the other.

Hedges and herb beds spring through homedeck, clematis and hazel, wild azalea, hyssop, and tansy, climbing hydrangea in the ramp- and stairwells, jasmine in halls and common rooms, the odors of earth and ivy cycling through the ventilation. It's the most desper-ately beautiful thing Arrigo knows and it can't be shared with Earth at all.

On their couch, intertwined, reading, his butt perched on Mike's feet, his amazing feet, broad and musclebound and lively as dogs, Arrigo asks, Is this perfect happiness?

Here is how he screws it all up.

THE SHIP HOLDS a town hall meeting in homedeck's auditorium. A long table of experts convene on stage, lit dramatically—Psychcomm is not above using an authoritative amber gel—and they share what's known about mass somato-melancholic events, or MSMEs. Since the first hypoxia event, there have been eleven more MSMEs: epi-sodes of widespread psychological and physical disturbance linked to dangerous biome imbalances. Several of these biome imbalances created hypoxic conditions, which account for some of the psycho-logical symptoms. But three MSMEs followed the reverse pattern, mass depressions leading to critical neglect of the biome, leading to blights, swarms, crop failures, with no clear biological or ecological first cause for them. It's these three that M.E. Park cites to support their theory of MSMEs as *relational* events.

The crew attending the town hall fill the concert auditorium's audience sections. Arrigo, in the orchestra seats, cranes and finds Lana in the balcony and watches for her reaction.

The MSMEs are critical occasions in our relatedness to Earth, M.E. says from their seat on stage. These events correspond to locally constructed temporalities and cosmographies: the last large body in the Solar System, the ten-year anniversary of launch, the one light-year mark. "Homesickness is not a sentimentality, but relational pathology," M.E. says. Lana listens out of the skeptical side of her face.

Arrigo catches Father Leo's eye, a few velvet rows back, and they trade grimaces. M.E. is a brilliant thinker, but an obscure public speaker. In the balcony seats, Lana opens a picture book and reads it quietly to her son on her lap.

The town hall opens for questions. Arrigo's knees crack as he stands. Mike shoots him a look and he answers with a reassuring gesture. He's got this.

He approaches the orchestra pit microphone with the expedition members' eyes on his back. "I'd like to give testimony."

The ship's captain, in the center of the table, tells him he has up to five minutes. She is a former Chinese Air Force colonel; instead of a uniform, she wears an olive blazer with epaulets. Arrigo isn't wholly prepared for those epaulets.

"As you know," Arrigo says, gesturing behind him, "our own Maestro Melsinger has just won a major prize on Earth for *La Traviata in the Amazon*."

Well: the tenses get tricky here. From one point of view, Melsinger's opera won two years before. There is a convention on the *Ekphrasis* to treat Earth news as happening when the signal reaches the ship—supposedly, this is the only sane meaning of simultaneity at a distance—but everyone knows better, everyone appreciates the irony of a current affairs upcast. The imperfect present must needs be imperfect; in any case, Melsinger has won, had won, did win a Pulitzer and when Arrigo says this, fevered applause breaks from the dozen opera die-hards.

Someone shouts Arrigo's name. He turns and gives a gracious nod and notes, entirely truthfully, that the libretto was definitely not what won. "Still, I was invested. Too much so, in fact."

Arrigo traces the eight years since they opened the finished opera on board the *Ekphrasis*, on this very stage: eight years for the score to tumble down the Vine and hit Earth, for Earth's opera houses to hustle donors, commission the work, and mount the "world" premiere, for the Pulitzer committee to vote and beam news of their award back up the Vine, and for that transmission to catch up to the ship. Every artist knows the misery of bracing for the public's reaction. But for that suspense to last *eight years*—in a way, he says, he's grateful for the data lag, because it forced him to confront how unhealthy his attention to Earth's reaction was. How miserable it made him, exactly like during a MSME. Anxious, self-doubting, boggy, and wretched, and for what? Are Earth's prizes even a relevant response to space art? Or has the *Ekphrasis* escaped their gravity too?

"You have one minute remaining," the captain says. But Arrigo is just warming up.

From the 1960s to 2010s, the dancer Marta Becket performed one-woman shows in a run-down theater in the California desert, the Amargosa Opera House in Death Valley Junction. Every night for fifty years she danced, almost always to an empty house. Nobody lived in Death Valley Junction anymore and nobody visited. So she painted herself an audience on the walls of the theater: royals and courtiers in their finery, in opera boxes, in rapt attention, as murals along the theater walls. A virtual audience.

"I propose Earth too is a virtual audience, something of a sentimental insanity." Arrigo raises his voice, meeting the panelists' impatient eyes but addressing the people seated behind him, one more angel of history blown by the past's wreckage into the future. "And maybe we'd be better off without it. Maybe if we're less attached to Earth's idea of us, we'll stop being so wretched and out of our minds every time there's a big anniversary or milestone."

Later, everyone will say this was the moment when Mike Faustino looked alarmed. Everyone will tell Arrigo how profoundly offended Melsinger was, chin tucking, face ashy and formal, and how silent the auditorium had fallen. But for now, Arrigo has still further to go.

"You are over your time, Mr. Durante." The captain's blazer is tailored so tight, she looks unbreathing, already a monument of herself.

Arrigo rehearses the arguments the coffee anarchists have made for a decade: That the Ekphrasis Foundation is hardly the charitable betterment-of-all-mankind project it styles itself as; that the ship beams down $1.2 billion worth of intellectual property every month; that copyrights and patents, Vine-platform advertising, and sheer cultural capital stand to enrich the Foundation's investors by hundreds of billions more.

"Sit *down*, Mr. Durante." She has no gavel; she slaps the table.

And who were those investors? A shadowy pharma concern that had bet the company on an anti-aging drug, which turned out so difficult to administer, it was all but unmarketable—that is, unless the *Ekphrasis* expedition made it look viable again. A space heavy industry group stalled on the edge of bankruptcy by buggy biomes and climate fatigue at home—that is, unless the *Ekphrasis* worked out the kinks of space travel and recaptured the public's sense of romance. Why should we scrape for these vultures? Why should our imagination, our labor, our lives serve the same rapacious capitalism that pushed our birth planet toward geo-collapse?

"We are almost two light-years from Earth, now," he says. "At this distance, the Oort cloud is shaped less by the Sun and planets than by the galactic tide—the combined gravity of the Milky Way. *Our* path ahead is shaped by the voice of every star in the galaxy. Maybe if we concentrate on those voices, these mass crises will finally stop."

He thanks the panel and sweeps up the aisle. No one makes a sound. Not that he expected applause—but whispering, consternation, ideally, the sound of a community beginning to change its mind. Still, this only proves his point: we need to let go of others' approval or disapproval and embrace that absolute silence that defines our life apart in the vacuum. He wanted to introduce the idea of this silence as a sort of qualm, which would grow into a yearning, until he, and Mike, and the rest of Father Leo's little group satisfied that yearning and cut the Vine for good.

FATHER LEO ROSENBAUM transitioned when he was young. By the time he entered the seminary, no one questioned his presentation. Just because gender is constructed doesn't mean it isn't also real, he likes to say. A house is constructed, but it's still a roof over your head. And gender is like a house, a kind of shelter we each inhabit. Jesus was born in a Bethlehem manger, a cave full of farm animals and straw bedding, because that's the best his parents could give him; but as a young *tektōn*, craftsman, he built himself a house in Capernaum. So, too, everyone builds their own shelter—which is gender, but also persona, creed, identity—out of the scraps they can scavenge or buy, and sometimes it looks like the house they were raised in, sometimes more like the house across the street, and sometimes it is totally unfamiliar, like the gender M.E. Park has constructed for themselves. For some, a childhood home is a source of strength, a happy memory carried forward; for others, like Jesus, a site of humility, a memory of poverty, persecution, and the need to escape.

Earth is a house of grief and secrets. Where Father Leo's Mother Church still schemes to annul his ordination, where his own parishioners spat at him. To Mike Faustino, he says: where your neighbors and classmates tormented you. To Arrigo, he says: where you hid yourself in the shadows of others' expectations. To his little group, he says: where you were abused, shamed, and raped to "fix" who you are. We left that home and built a new shelter in the stars. Even if we didn't rivet the girders and hammer the plating ourselves, we build it every day with our labor, our imagination, and our very breath. And there is a Voice accompanying us, he tells them, unlike any voice on Earth. A Voice in the wilderness, calling to us from out of the Deep—if only we can secure the silence to hear it.

Arrigo, for all his distaste for religion, is ready to believe in Leo's Voice, because he has heard it, too. It slips into his poems as he works them, if he's quiet. The line wants a word; the assonance implies it, the meter races toward it, but he can't think of it; then something passes behind him and dreams the word into seed. It's not God, this Voice, but the planet Qaf itself. The hope of it, a theory of home, a center away from Earth. A belonging outside belonging.

He and Father Leo were the first to champion M.E. Park's relational model of MSMEs. Arrigo grasped the shape of it at once: alienation and exile peaking across biotic communities. (*The birds mourn with you, Orpheus, the crowds of wild animals, the hard flints; the gathered trees tear out their hair.*) And Father Leo saw in it the nature of his ministry at last. He knew a thing or two about leaving every familiar construct behind to race toward an uncertain peace; his experiences would help shepherd this earthless people into being. Which meant— lucky him—*Deus vult*, God wills it.

But the Biocomm scientists were appalled by what they saw as M.E.'s magical thinking, and M.E. was unwilling to press a theory they'd barely begun to develop. So, Leo formed a study group of sympathetic minds. This little group has quietly concluded that Earth is the problem, that the crew's attachment to Earth is causing MSMEs, and that it will take a clean break—Vine severance—to stop them.

Our survival requires we embrace our nature as outsiders, Leo says. Queers, free thinkers, anti-consumerists—whatever our axis of difference, we're different. He indicates the tattoo on Mike's arm. "The canyon tree frog doesn't waste time trying to be a bullfrog; it doesn't get torn up inside because it doesn't thrive everywhere, but fights to thrive within its own way of being. We're on this ship because we fit *here*. But we are getting bombarded by bullfrog thinking every second. Maybe that's fine for the bullfrogs, and maybe it isn't. Maybe feeling like you have to have two kids, two cars, a grass lawn all winter, and a steak dinner every night to be happy is what got Earth into such a bad state. What I do know is that that kind of thinking on this ship will literally kill us."

"And if it doesn't kill us, it makes us miserable," Mike says. "We're fixated on what we're not, what we can't ever be, and I'm sick of it. It needs to stop, and if people can't find the strength to throw off their own chains, well, hand me the fucking bolt cutters."

Arrigo has his misgivings. Sabotage is undemocratic. He'd prefer to build consensus. This puts priest and partner alike in an awkward spot.

"Democracy has rarely been a friend to us," Mike tells him.

Father Leo tells him, "Majority rule only gives people the illusion of self-determination here. They're still serving old masters, old ways of thinking. Being outside majorities is part of our gift—it's what queerness *is*."

They thought they had him convinced. He said he was. Then Arrigo decided to give hearts and minds a fair chance to come around and stepped up to the town hall microphone.

"LOOK, I WAS careful. I think that went well," he tells Mike, after. "It may take some time, but people will start seeing it our way. They'll review their experiences and start noticing what we noticed, especially if there's another MSME." Arrigo pronounces it *miss-me*, something he'd started years ago, to drive home the role of Earth-attachment.

They are in a long corridor on homedeck. Over two decades, the *Ekphrasis* artists and craftspeople have taken apart the framed prints and Earth-kitsch that cluttered these corridors and repurposed them.

Biome engineers have replaced them with potted herbs and creeping vines. The morning glories Lana uprooted from the rainforest—
they are maddeningly invasive—now string through the halls leading
to Arrigo and Mike's quarters. The plants are oxygen insurance; no
one is taking any chances with another MSME. Constant winds push
and tumble through the halls, hyper-ventilating; the weather artists aren't taking chances either.

"If there's another MSME," Mike says, "someone will die."

And this is true: they have both lost people. A cellist with asthma
suffocated in xer bed. Mike's friend Klaus, the one Arrigo called
Ragged Klaus, is dead by his own hand.

Scuttling across the floors of silent seas

"And if the biome collapses," Mike continues, "we all die."

"I get it. We can't wait for everyone to sign on. But what about
some more people?"

The vines and herbs along the wall shake in the driving winds,
trembling like puppies, their stems hard and exhausted.

The plan depends on looking like an accident, Mike says. "I don't
want to spend the next however-many years a pariah for cutting the
Vine. Babe—that speech was a disaster."

"Oh, come on. I was subtle."

"I love you, but you are not subtle. Nothing about you is subtle,
OK? I don't know where you get that idea." Mike rests his forehead
on Arrigo's chest and breathes deeply. "We'll push back the time-
line. And hope no one notices the thing."

Behind Mike is a fern, and behind that, a painting that used to
be a moose drinking knee-deep from a brook, but which has since

been painted over as a green and white abstract. Arrigo sees only triangles and swirls in it. Mike sees a shipwreck on a lighthouse.

La Traviata in Space

It's been years since I've sent a vinecast, but I still record them. Like Marta dancing for her painted audience, some part of me still gestures toward the crowd I've renounced. My lizard brain—the lizard poet. The suspicion that my poems are still, mysteriously, "for" something. That they have use, can be instrumental. Continuing *this* project is particularly pointless, given that Melsinger's opera is finished: Why keep talking about *La Traviata*? It's not my favorite opera. It's not my favorite Verdi opera. It's not even my favorite of Verdi's *middle* operas. But there's something lovely and defiant about pointlessness. Pointlessness is poetry, it's queerness, a commitment of everything we are to a pursuit whose only end is its own perfect execution.

In the lead-up to D-Day, Allied communications used the Symbolist poems of Paul Verlaine to coordinate the French Resistance: when the British broadcast the opening lines of *"Chanson d'automne,"*

> *Les sanglots longs*
> *Des violons*
> *De l'automne*

That meant: "Allied forces will invade Normandy in two weeks' time." Twelve days later, when the French heard the following verse,

> *Blessent mon coeur*
> *D'une longeur*
> *Monotone*

That meant: "Operation Overlord begins in 48 hours, commence rail sabotage operations."

There's a violent, magnificent irony in this, in how little Verlaine wanted his poems to "mean," to be "for" anything but language itself. The Symbolists celebrated obscurity, dream imagery, "significant pleonasms, mysterious ellipses, outstanding anacoluthia, any audacious and multiform surplus." Above all, avoid direct meaning: "Keep away," Verlaine wrote, "from the murderous Sharp Saying."

THE NEXT DAY, Lana is at his door, knocking with the toe of her work boot. She holds Elkeid asleep against her shoulder. Elkeid is helplessly unconscious, rosebud lips murmuring in his star-baby language. Technically, Elkeid is twelve, but he has the body of a small six-year-old. The vitacene he absorbed from twenty-seven months in Lana's womb will flush out in another three years, at which point he should age normally. Lana transfers her son over the threshold into Arrigo's arms. Technically, Elkeid is his son too. But the significance of these technicalities remains an open question between the two couples—Lana and her second wife, Penny; Arrigo and his don't-call-us-husbands, Mike.

"Big date planned?" Arrigo asks in a stage whisper. "Dinner and dancing?"

"Fucking and sleeping," Lana says grimly. "I know my limits."

Arrigo is happy to watch Elkeid whenever Lana needs a break from him, and Lana's great virtue is knowing when she needs a break. Elkeid is a handful; when he's not a handful, he is a terror; when he's not a terror, he is a sphinx. There are a few star-babies on the ship now and they are all strange, furtive, changeling children, made more of starlight and void than of Earth. Developmentally, who knows where they are: Elkeid isn't twelve or six or something in between but the whole range at once. His interior life is illegible. Like hearing a poem in an untranslated language: you can only enjoy the words' musical quality. Arrigo is endlessly fascinated and the two spend hours in nonsense dialogues, probing each other's unaccountable minds.

Motherhood wears Lana raw. It strips her of her formidable competence and drags her into the better person she has to be. Whereas the speechlessness of ecosystems brings out in her a certain softness and receptivity, people she tends to steamroll. People are a battle of wills Lana will always win, secure and abrupt in her knowing-better. Elkeid demands both modes from her. He is as wordless and alien as a beehive but, unlike a beehive, unlike a mangrove or moss, he cannot be relied on to execute basic survival programs without her enforcing them, like, say, eating enough food to sustain caloric requirements. ("You'd think, a human child being a more sophisticated organism than moss, he could do that. But you'd be wrong.") Arrigo gets a perverse thrill from being a little better at something than Lana; and in this secret, silly rivalry, he is very much a father.

"He's not out for the whole night, is he?" Arrigo says. He supports Elkeid's seat and with his free hand maneuvers the child's noodle arms over his shoulder. "Mike wants to try Narnia."

"Where is Mike? When do you think he'll be back?"

Lana doesn't quite meet his eyes.

Mike is finishing a shift at the communal kitchens so they can eat take-out tonight. Lana follows Arrigo into the living room. She stops and squares her stance in a way that makes Arrigo stop, too.

"Here's the deal," she says.

"Uh-oh."

"Two chances. I'll give you two chances—because I know you'll waste the first one—"

"Do you want tea? I don't think we have tea . . ." Arrigo spins into the second bedroom, waltzing Elkeid and talking over his shoulder. "I should put him down, shouldn't I? This sounds like a conversation."

"—two chances to come clean about whatever you're planning. Whatever that crazy speech was for. Right now, no bullshitting."

Arrigo lays Elkeid in his small, high bed. Elkeid's quilt is cotton, flimsy from use, hand-stitched in dinosaurs. Arrigo tucks it under the boy's pearl chin.

"I don't know what you're talking about."

"That's one," Lana warns. She is in the doorway, backlit. "I'm not playing around."

Arrigo straightens. He says, "Please don't talk to me like you don't take me seriously."

Lana holds up her hands in apology. In the dark, it's a creak of her beat-up leather jacket. "Fair," she says. "I've given my life for this expedition, is all I'm saying."

They argue in whispers, like trees argue, two long-lived beings so tangled at the roots they already know everything the other has to say. Neither of them moves to leave the bedroom. Easier to do this darkly, wrapped in the hum of the ship. Arrigo lays out his arguments knowing they will fail to sway her: he explains Earth-attachment and bullfrog thinking and the long shadow of people who've refused the gift of us. It sounds much dumber spoken out loud to a skeptic. Lana answers carefully; she is trying not to steamroll him, and he is grateful for that effort, even as he hears her self-restraint cracking.

Their voices climb. Arrigo's takes on a shrill, plaintive sound he finds humiliating. "Lana, Lana, please, oh, Christ, will you listen—"

"I can *hear* you fine," Lana says. "It's just that what you're saying is nonsense."

"Sorry," Arrigo says awfully. He is always stepping in ableist cowpies around her. "I didn't mean it that way."

Lana relents. "Let me rephrase. I *consider*, in *my* view, what you are saying," she says, "to be. Nonsense."

She sets her hands on her hips and sighs. Well, she tried.

"*Nostalgia* was a medical diagnosis, originally, did you know that?" Arrigo says. "An incapacitating heartsickness, *mal du Suisse*. Swiss mercenaries in the seventeenth century who'd spent too much time abroad experienced fever, fainting, palpitations, lesions—sometimes they died of it. Rousseau says soldiers were whipped for singing the *Ranz des vaches* because of the inconsolable yearning for alpine pastures it inspired."

"Are you fucking serious right now? The seventeenth century?"

Arrigo folds to the floor, criss-cross-applesauce. It's exhausting, holding his own against her. Lana checks the bed guiltily; she is letting herself get too loud. But Elkeid is asleep.

"I'm not saying there's nothing to what you're saying." Lana is trying again to cool herself down. "If you'd written this in a poem—"

"Come on. Why do you think that's a concession?"

"Arrigo. You're asking me to give up the whole point of this mission, for the scientists at least, which is to share our results with Earth. We have sixty more years of biospherics research before we even get to Qaf and *then* there's everything from the planet itself. And you're telling me I have to cut myself off from everyone who could review and develop that research at home? No way. I'm sorry, but no.

Science is a community; it has to be. So, yeah, I'm going to need you to be more fucking rigorous than that. Not woo-woo self-help stuff, OK? Give me data, give me peer-reviewed models, Jesus, when you're proposing to cut people's entire connection to home without even any warning, without their—" She stops herself.

She won't say it. She is still too proud.

"Consent," he says.

"Consent," she admits.

It's a rule that neither of them talk about the night they spent together on her psilocybin mushrooms—about the technicality of Elkeid's conception. The last time they talked it out, they didn't speak for a year. Consent is a tender word. All he said was he felt they'd been careless with his state of mental existence at the time and all she heard was *you Lana Malouf are a rapist.* This is the peril of carrying new problems in old vessels. Received forms can't begin to articulate how a stoned faggot's desire for a hot butch in a suit is something more and less than wanting to have sex with her. But desires get scrambled; bodies commit category errors. That's not exactly a violation, not a violation *she* committed, not in the way that word is used. The shame Arrigo feels has more to do with the collapse of their hard-won queernesses in the shadow of some biological agenda (whose?) to conceive Elkeid.

She'd spent most of her pregnancy estranged. She wouldn't talk to him, and Mike didn't want him talking to her either. Carolyn dumped her for cheating. Arrigo couldn't stand it. Her labor was hard, obviously. On the second day, she let him inside the delivery room, and he climbed into the bed and held her shoulders for thirteen hours, intent on witnessing this creative blood magic he was and wasn't part of. Lana soaked him in sweat. He saw her shit and cry. She promised desperately she'd take more care; she promised she would never steamroll him again into anything and promised to re-promise when she wasn't splitting open, so he'd know she meant it. She did mean it, and he did know it.

But we're only human, and Earth is Earth.

Lana asks him, "How old is Mike, do you think—physically?"

Arrigo looks up; he adds and divides on his lips. "About 34 or 35?"

"Does he look 34 or 35?" Lana asks. She joins Arrigo on the floor and settles her hands on his knees. "I mean, he sure doesn't look 47. He's got amazing skin, he takes care of himself. But—how many tattoos has he lost?"

Arrigo is silent. His own body has lost a good amount of its therapeutic ink. He hasn't looked at Lana's back recently, but twenty years of vitacene micro-doses means about a quarter of her manticore should have broken down and disappeared. He frowns.

"What are you saying?"

Elkeid's quilts shift. The boy sits up in his bed. "Is Mike home?"

Lana lifts Arrigo to his feet. "If there's a problem with Mike's absorption of the vitacene—you know, the drug our corporate masters developed, the one *they* have all the research and trial data for—then Mike needs the Vine more than any of us."

From the front door, the sounds of keys, locks tumbling, the metal tongue retracting. Lana kisses Arrigo on the forehead. "Do the right thing, and we'll keep him out of it."

When they step, blinking, into the living room and its dreamy bronze light, Arrigo's face has lost its color, and his lids tighten as if staring into the Sun.

.   .   .

MIKE WALKS IN, balancing stacked containers of lentils and salads in the crook of an arm, shaking his keys out of the lock with his free hand. Arrigo scrutinizes the man he loves with new attention. Mike has lost some of his attractive babyfat, his high cheekbones now sharp and feline, his features taut, distinguished. His gold-brown face is unwrinkled—except, Arrigo notices, the lovely crows' feet around his eyes. His hair is black and thick as ever—except his hairline is creeping back at the wings. It's inconclusive. Mike is in that expanse from thirty to fifty that means only he is a beautiful man, not an overgrown boy. He returns Arrigo's attention quizzically, then musters a smile for Lana. His tree frog tattoo is unfaded. The funny sigil on the back of his neck is unbroken. Arrigo has a mental map of Mike's body, of the knots, vines, animals, dinosaurs, and words inked on his partner, which in turn map out the life remaining to him, or should, if they worked. As he embraces Mike, he breathes in the scent of his hair oil and his fingers slip under Mike's shirt to touch the figures along his ribs, all complete, Arrigo already knows. Maybe a smudge gone here and there, enough for Arrigo to lie to himself.

"What's wrong?" Mike says. His dark eyes, their lashes, all concern.

"I—" Arrigo stammers. He looks back at Lana feebly.

And so what if Mike is aging naturally? Arrigo's love isn't shallow. So what if Mike grows old ahead of him, if he dies before him. They will still have their life together. That's all anyone can ask. So what if Arrigo, rounding forty-five as Mike hits his mid-eighties, ends up changing Mike's diapers, feeding him oxygen, witnessing the slow, humiliating decimation of the person most precious to him, while Arrigo is in his prime. So what if senility, bone loss, and arthritis turn his lover into a kind of grandfather instead.

"There's something I have to take care of," Arrigo says, then grabs his own keys. He wheels back and kisses Mike deeply.

HERE IS HOW you clip a Vine: The relay transponders that make up the chain—don't call them satellites, because they don't orbit anything—are extremely directional, they have to point their antennae precisely at the links ahead and behind them to transmit and receive. But they're not all in a line, otherwise the ones released at higher speeds plow into the ones released during the deceleration phase, not to mention the ship. Instead, they're nudged to one side at angles when released, so in addition to speeding ahead, they're drifting apart. That makes for constant chatter along the Vine, each link telling its neighbors, "Here I am! I'm this way!" and tracking their positions. And on the ship, there's a master process keeping tabs on each link, helping them see one another, like a mother duck checking on her ducklings behind her, and sitting above that mother duck process in the ship's computer are the guardian processes, double-checking the links' position data against simulations and correcting rounding errors and signal noise.

But suppose you have a way to feed the guardian processes spoofed data. Suppose you've convinced them the orienting protocols of the last four links in the Vine are corrupted, requiring persistent correction. Now suppose you could, one day, pull a trigger that fools the guardians into sending a correction so extreme, those ducklings get turned around so badly that they lose a bead on their neighbors and the ship. You've got the last four transponders unable to receive or send a signal, shouting helplessly, "I'm here! I'm this way!" in the wrong direction, into open space.

Arrigo lays it all out for the captain and the ship's marshal. The marshal presses him to name names, but he gives only his own—and Father Leo's, that can't be helped. Leo's "Little Group" is an open secret on the ship, although there's no definite sense of its membership. Some artists, some scientists, some of Mike's anarchist friends from the café co-op. The sculptress and former kirtan singer, Jayne, who converted to Buddhism and sees Earth-attachment as *upādāna*. The LGs are tolerated as one more oddball utopian club on a ship with no lack of utopians. Like the café co-op itself, or Jayne's group of trans and nonbinary nuns, who call themselves nones.

"Not every LG knew about the plan," Arrigo says. "Leo and I formed the Very Little Group to carry out the sabotage. It's him and me . . ." He trails off, hearing how implausible that is.

". . . and at least one other person who can code telecom satellites," the captain says. "We have to assume that's your husband, don't we?"

"Don't call us husbands," he says automatically. "Don't call them satellites. It was—it was Ragged Klaus. He programmed the trigger before he died in the last MSME. Check his file, he could code."

The captain and marshal exchange a look of skepticism. Arrigo is unafraid. Fear is for beings with futures to worry over. He is a flower retching color into the dark: pointless, complete in his small moment. The captain thanks him for his change of heart and lets him go.

He takes the long way back to his quarters. He loiters in Hall Q, watching hologram-Qaf shudder and reform in its mist. The pampas are gone, the mountains are seas, his favorite geography keeps losing out to new spectral data and now he is afraid. Maybe he'll explain himself to Mike and Mike will never forgive him. Maybe there is no fix for Mike's vitacene dosing. Change, heartbreak—Arrigo is barreling into them as fast as any other creature in time.

Qaf is always updating. Concrescing, M.E. would say. Modulating, Melsinger would say. "Dying," Arrigo says, then asks himself why.

His skin crawls. Someone has walked over my grave.

He picks up oxygen candles as he hurries home. He gets the last two in the box. Not a good sign.

He enters the compartment softly. Mike is on the floor with Elkeid between his legs, reading aloud. Their backs face him. Lana is still there, pretending to read her phone. Her eyes flick to meet his. The book is *The Lion, the Witch, and the Wardrobe*. They stop every other sentence and Mike explains lions, and children going to stay in country estates during the Blitz. He explains cities, bombs, houses, airplanes, and trains. What the countryside is and why there are no bombs there. Elkeid follows along, but seems taxed. What's snow? he asks. I don't get it. Mike explains snow and winter. They have been through this before. Mike or Arrigo or Lana will explain snow, or oceans, and Elkeid will understand and promptly forget. The concepts don't stick because he is indifferent to them. They are as irrelevant and difficult as the multiplication tables he also refuses to learn.

Arrigo steps forward, braced to be honest. "Hi, there . . ."

But before he gets any further, Lana stands, staring from her phone to Arrigo. "I thought you took care of it," she says, paling. "Arrigo—the Vine's just gone dead."

Mike looks between the two of them, more alert to tone than meaning. Understanding breaks across his face: what Arrigo has done, and what roles Lana and even Elkeid must have played in what

Arrigo has done. Mom, Dad, and the kid: a tidy nuclear family, nuking him all over again.

La Traviata in Space

She'd been a first-class soprano when Verdi was nobody. They found each other in Paris, fortunes nimbly reversed, his star ever rising, her voice ruined from overwork, and they made good use of Parisian discretion. When Verdi settled on the outskirts of Busetto, his hometown, Giuseppina Strepponi came with him. The scandal of her presence was too great for the Busettani. 'La Strepponi' was an actress, a celebrity, meaning she was a whore; she'd had four illegitimate children by her agents and impresarios and had exhibited herself on stage while pregnant, delivering one child hours after curtain calls. For Verdi to live openly with this woman, unmarried, in the sight of his dead wife's family, who had done so much to nurture his early career—how could the good people of Busetto tolerate it? They didn't dare offend him directly, but to Giuseppina they were openly cruel. She did not leave the house except to attend church, alone, where the congregation left a wide, empty circle around her in the pews.

That image haunts me: the pious emptiness around her. In *La Traviata's* second act, Violetta's confrontation with Germont—when Alfredo's genteel father persuades Violetta to leave Alfredo to avoid a scandal—clearly draws something from Giuseppina's experience in Busetto, with Antonio Barezzi, Verdi's beloved mentor and father-in-law, as a model for Germont. "You live in a town with the bad habit of getting mixed up in other people's affairs, and disapproving of everything that does not conform to its own ideas," Verdi wrote to Barezzi. "Who knows what our relations are? What affairs? What ties? Who knows whether she is my wife or not?"

("*Think—even the sweetest feelings will be no balm,*" Germont warns Violetta, "*because these bonds are not blessed by Heaven. Oh, give up this seductive dream . . .*")

Giuseppina couldn't fail to sense that field of revulsion, bridging whatever distance the Busettani set between themselves and her. Like I can feel your revulsion, O people of Earth, even light-years away. With the Vine silent, and all the chatter cleared, the flattery and vitriol gone, I hear it stronger—our opposition, the way our respective edges will always grind on each other. Come on, don't get offended. It's a collective "you." You whose bonds are blessed by Heaven. We've always known your contempt. Even the queers with loving homes, friends, who live in cities with Pride parades, yes, even the ones who pass, yes—*oh, give up this seductive dream*—it's that keenness of difference that pricks us to self-censor. To wear costumes of intense sameness, or intense distinction. Do you know what the bullfighter's costume is called? *Traje de luces*, a suit of lights. Costumes to dazzle, bewilder, and survive.

Once Violetta has left Alfredo and gone back to Paris—back to her old protector—Verdi opens the next scene with a masque. The women take up Spanish fans and perform a "gypsy dance," then the men grab capes and do a matador dance. These are hired entertainers, or, in the staging I prefer, it's the high-society revelers themselves, playacting as hot-blooded, free-roaming Iberians. Actual Romani in Paris were outcasts, of course. Like Violetta herself, the Roma's standing at this party is contingent on her entertainment value. In the same way, the Busettani could enjoy Giuseppina Strepponi on stage while ostracizing her in church; in a sense, this is necessary, the pleasure of watching her perform depends at least in part on the satisfaction that she is excluded from respectable society.

In evolutionary biology, most theories for why queerness persists, despite no direct reproductive advantage, propose that we are still in some way *useful* to procreation. We're helpers in the nest; we buffer out aggressive sexual competition; we do hair and makeup, foster dogs, keep women's soccer afloat; we make over clueless husbands to help them impress their wives. And I'm sorry, but that's fucking bleak. I don't accept that we exist for the pleasure of, and at the convenience of, our normal brothers and sisters. Count me out.

WHEN TROUBLE COMES again, it comes by the birds. Their numbers increase without clear cause. Too much food, or habitat, or another mindless peaking event in a complex ecosystem. Timing is mysterious: it's been two months since the Vine cut out and the crew sank into grief. Lana hears wild, unearthly calls throughout the forest during dark-cycle. Mike frees doves trapped in access tunnels. Greendeck's artificial winds, tumbling through the ship's rotations, tangle and merge into ferocious windballs that tear off branches, snatch birds out of their flight, and fling them around the ship. Sparrows spiral down the greening halls of homedeck and roost in the creepers. Remy NDiaye wakes, scrambles to turn on the light, and finds a panicking magpie crashing across his ceiling.

Birdsong floods into the silence left by the Vine, but it's a desperate, senseless music—not nature's exuberance but its solipsism, shrieking to hear itself shriek, a child scaring herself making faces into a mirror.

Remy and his polycule wear all black with ocean-blue armbands; M.E. Park wears all white. Memorials paper the halls. For some, it's easier to think of everyone on Earth as dead now, this is the only sane meaning of bereavement at a distance. Others imagine the ones they left behind as forever alive, unkillable in silence. There are support groups. There are meetings every Wednesday at six. Jayne's nones hold loss meditations on the beach of the reef habitat. Vine severance has transformed them: Jayne has shaved her hair, her long, precious hair, and everyone is startled by how seriously they take the nones' serenity in detachment. Now would be a good time for a priest, maybe. But Leo is in the brig, and he is no longer a priest.

It was one of the last messages to come up the Vine: a letter from Rome, his ordination is annulled and Leo excommunicated. Even the bishop who ordained him is laicized, apparently on photographic evidence that Leo was clockable as a deacon. *Thou art a priest forever,* except you never were. Every Mass he has said is retroactively emptied of meaning. Every sin he has absolved relapses; every Host he has slipped on to trusting tongues is bread, just bread.

Two months after Father Leo is arrested, the bird population explodes. They wipe out the earthworms and pollinators in a handful of days. They get sucked into the ventilation ducts and foul the fans. The ship braces for hypoxic conditions at a time when the biome most needs clear-thinking humans.

Lana puts it to Biocomm and Psychcomm simply: "If we can't restore viable pollinator and nutrient cycler communities, the farms will collapse, and we will starve."

The committees crowd into the bedroom of M.E. Park, whose cancer treatments have made them too weak to attend meetings. Everyone is baggy with hopelessness and bitterness. The reserve oxygen candles are gone; homedeck zones with blocked ventilation must evacuate. They will have to ration food stores preemptively.

M.E.'s oxygen equipment cuts the room's silence into whirs, clicks, and sighs. Arrigo stares at it, unspeakably tempted.

Lana leans against the wall, arms crossed, one foot cocked against the baseboard, and Arrigo, hunched on the floor, leans his head against her ankle. He dogs her everywhere now, her faithful, half-competent assistant. His hair is a bird's nest of sweat, seed, and dirt. He has tried being on his own, sufficient in himself. He has failed and he hates it. Lana's death-stare protects him from the poisonous looks everyone throws him, this room no exception.

The maddening part is, the Vine's death wasn't even his fault. The sabotage never happened. Opscomm scrubbed the navigation software and two months of health chatter show no lost relay links. Maybe everyone blames him for what he was willing to do, though, and connects that to what has happened. But what *has* happened? The problem must lie further down the chain. Maybe Earth itself stopped transmitting. And that prospect is so much more terrible than voluntarily cutting the Vine, it's hard to even look at it straight on. If the Foundation had run out of money and folded, there would have been some warning. A goodbye message, if nothing else. Good luck, weirdos. Sashay away. But an abrupt silence—it implies—

The ship is in no state to work out what it implies. Either Earth has become a crueler place than they thought possible, or the planet has fallen into worse shape than anyone imagined.

Maybe that's what everyone blames Arrigo for. Not the sabotage plot, but the scales of loss its failure has forced them to contemplate.

M.E.'s oxygen tube makes them the clearest thinker on the ship. "We've done this before," they remind the committees. "We are a part of this biome—we have a function, we're good at it, and we'll do it again—"

"We will starve," Lana says, shaking her head.

M.E.'s oxygen compressor whirs, clicks, and sighs, like a bamboo water fountain trickling and ducking in a shaded Japanese garden.

On greendeck, Lana teaches house cats how to hunt birds. The ship's veterinarians keep a list of cats left fertile and together they are breeding a feral colony to control the birds, but in the meantime, the biome needs predators. These indoor cats are lazy, spoiled animals, but they retain their original instructions, or echoes of them, somewhere behind those dragon-eyes, and anyway the birds are quite stupid, easy prey when they're out of balance with their ecosystem. Like they know they're supposed to be eaten, that's their purpose now, to sing and perish. Lana practically picks them off the trees like figs. She screws their little necks and dances their little bodies from strings in front of the house cats, cooing, Kitty kitty kitty.

She would bring down the little birds.
And I would bring down the little birds.

Arrigo and Elkeid follow behind, climbing trees and stealing eggs.

There is something graceful and girlish in how Elkeid moves through the overstory, picking his nimble way, branch to branch, nest to nest, across the synapses between live oaks, singing in his nonsense language. There is a sensation Arrigo has when he wakes suddenly out of deep dreaming, when the mind rushes into itself and the soup of images and emotion snaps into the specifics of a person, a particular consciousness. Elkeid's mind seems to exist in the moment before that snap. He anticipates that precision of self without quite leaving the chaos of dreams. Elkeid will drop out of the tree's crown when he's finished, without warning, never doubting he'll be caught. They lose half the eggs he's collected when he does this.

"I'd like to start Elkeid on voice lessons," Arrigo tells Lana that evening, at the dinner table. Dinner is fried robin's eggs over rice and one sweet potato. Lana chews blankly, not even pretending to listen. She's half-asleep and smells like small creatures' blood. Arrigo looks from her to her wife, Penny. "With your permission."

He is the helper in the nest. He exists to enhance the prospects of this incomprehensible son who drives them all to desperation. He is bad at it, but then no one is *good* at it. No one else has paid attention to Elkeid's singing, for example.

Penny is the ship's dentist, a necessary, dire person, high femme in a diamond way, who has never liked Arrigo, and now uses the Vine's failure as grounds to detest him openly. Arrigo feels for her. In her position, he'd also be appalled at Lana harboring him, letting him sleep on their sofa, sitting him at their table. This does not prevent him from accepting these graces, but he joins Penny in hating himself as a show of solidarity.

The lintel of the café co-op now reads *FUCK YOU ELGIES*. Arrigo and Mike have been banned for life. Caffeine withdrawal on top of the ugliest of break-ups: not recommended.

There's a vitacene zit growing on Penny's cheek, which he can't stop staring at. It's huge and yellow like a bruise; it has its own capillary system. She sees him gawking. They are two precious breaths away from strangling each other.

"Was this potato grown from dead expedition members?" Elkeid asks his mother. He tilts another bite into his mouth.

"What? No, my love," she says. She regards her son with weary, persistent unrecognition.

"Corpses are recycled, right? Into mulch. There were those suicides. And that man who overdosed on the stolen morphine."

His name comes from the star Eta Ursa Majoris, whose Arabic name is *Elkeid* or *Alkaid*, the leader of the daughters of the bier. Picture the Big Dipper: the bowl is the funeral bier and the three stars of its handle are the mourning maidens following it, Elkeid, Mizar, and Alioth.

"Cadavers aren't composted in the agricultural zones," Lana says. "Probably in the mangroves."

Arrigo, who swims in the mangrove swamp, imagines the dead peeking at him through the orchids' lewd eyes.

"Penny, I've always wondered—why *do* dentists have such high suicide rates?" Arrigo asks. He can't see Penny's tattoos, but pictures her clavicle tangled in barbed wire. "Are mouths really that disgusting?"

"I know one mouth that makes me want to die."

Mouths are where all the abominations of the human condition lie, Arrigo thinks. Me and my big mouth, he thinks.

Lana's fork travels automatically; when it taps a hunk of tuber against her teeth, she looks down and rediscovers she's eating. Her mind is two light-years away, on what she has lost.

HERE IS THE story of the tattoo on Leo's ribs, of St. Anthony tormented by devils. When Leo was a little atheist girl in the throes of dysphoria, he had as his tablet background a famous painting of St. Anthony's temptation: a swarm of monsters biting, pulling, and clawing at the desert hermit, lifting him into the sky, while the graybeard saint regards them with weary patience just this side of irritated. Leo took wisdom from this odd sense of a *tempting*, and solace in the saint's lack of alarm. In seminary, Leo realized how right he'd been to identify his despair with these diabolical forces, after D.C. Schindler's notion of *diabolon*, δια-βάλλω, a "throwing asunder" or "setting at odds"—the voices that seek to divide humans from God, act from potency, passion from reality. Voices of self-negation and cynicism. *Vade retro*.

Away in the brig, the birds' screams blow through the ventilation ducts and Leo re-reads the letter from Rome. Excommunication is a medicinal penalty, he is reminded. The Holy See's anxious hope is that Leo repent and return to the spiritual fold. (As a layman, the message makes clear; and as a woman.) It's not like he's surprised, though maybe he is a little, after all there was that one priest who'd had gender confirmation surgery and lived out the rest of her life without being laicized. There was a part of him, a cringing, fond part of him, that wondered if the Church he loved and served would graciously let him think he was still a priest. If only the Vine had failed before the message was sent, he could have continued as "Father" Leo. But that's not true. He would have known. Those diabolical voices, quiet for decades, whisper again from behind his thoughts: Isn't it time you gave up this pretense? This affectation, this subterfuge, this artifice, this parody, this spectacle, this beggar's opera. Leo's abjection is a thesaurus. Every word is needed to articulate how wrong and wayward Unfathered Leo is, how embarrassingly off course. What could be more trans than that? His priesthood like his maleness, both misguided hobbyisms taken too far. Leo listens to the birds and knows this is part of the MSME. An echo, a dream of a fight he has already won. *Vade retro.* Nevertheless.

Despair is an abyss without bottom, Thomas Merton wrote. *Do not think to close it by consenting to it and trying to forget you have consented.*

His plan was sound. In deep space, in the night-wilderness, he could develop a solitary language for God, apart from the institution that would inevitably reject him. Merton again: *The Desert Fathers believed that the wilderness had been created as supremely valuable in the eyes of God precisely because it had no value to men.* But, Leo is discovering, there is a wilderness still deeper and emptier than space.

This, then, is our desert: to live facing despair, and not to consent.

ACROSS THE SHIP, crew members shirk their work shifts, gorge their rations, and lie ashamed in bed with the lights off. Caloric restrictions and stale air make people catastrophic and petulant. There is no such thing as night and day, they think, the light-dark cycles are artificial, so why not sleep their way into starvation.

"Fucking children," Lana growls to no one. She pictures eating the meat off their fingers.

There's something to M.E.'s relational theories after all. Lana could feel the loss of Earth in her pelvis, like a gear shift; in her eyeteeth, like a tinnitus cutting out. For all they know, they are the only humans left in the universe. She wanted empirical evidence, didn't she? What could be more empirical than a kick in the gut? There's Qaf still to hope for, Arrigo reminds her loyally—they've taken up their old tango of mutual dependency—some crew members even want to revisit the no-settlement mandate. That's the wrong answer, though. If it's not the Mars relay link knocked out by an asteroid or planetary occlusion, if Earth's humans really have screwed up their own closed biome so bad they can't work a radio telescope, then the only moral course is to blow up the *Ekphrasis* before humans get anywhere near another planet with life.

The captain starts relocating crew members in low-ventilation areas to greendeck. In some cases, they are literally carried out of their beds and dumped in the grass. But their heavy grief doesn't lift. The dread and wretchedness persist despite greendeck's plentiful oxygen, and the afflicted sprawl on the turf, lost, hopeless, and obscure.

In the brig, Unfathered Leo presses his palmheels against his eyes until he sees stars. This is his prisoner's-cell window. The starlight outside is the dizziness inside him.

At Lana's instruction, Arrigo joins the team cleaning birdstrikes from the ducts. He needs a break from greendeck, anyway, from the birds' apocalyptic songs. And in a fatal turn of events, it's Mike Faustino who, without speaking or looking at him, leads him into the hot kidneys of the ship, to the water treatment pools. Here, ventilation is mission-critical: without oxygen, the secondary waste treatment won't work and their water cycle will fall out of rhythm, too. It reeks like the pits of Hell here, not the smell of death but of grotesque life, its excrescence. The shit of twenty-five hundred souls, or 2,433 souls, now. Arrigo, scrubbing fanblades, notices a tattoo on his forearm is newly fading. It's an abstract design, copied lovingly from Wright's Coonley window at the Art Institute in Chicago. The sight of its peaceful sephiroth of circles and grid, catching out of the corner of his eye, has never failed to transport him back to that time, that city, that building of wonders, an attack of youth and optimism. The thought that this memory-magic will break down with the ink's vanishing and these spontaneous doses of enthusiasm will decline out of his life is intolerable. He doesn't realize he's scrutinizing Mike until he hears him snap, "What now," and he hears himself ask if Mike's tattoos have faded. Which is to ask: Are you dying? Which is to ask: Am I going to die?

Mike lifts his oil-smudged t-shirt. Along the winged, silky crease over his pelvic bone, Our Lady of Guadalupe is losing her shoulder. So that's something. Both men are quiet. In another heartbeat, Arrigo is on his knees and Mike is roughing him around grabbing his hair in fistfuls and stabbing his dick down Arrigo's throat. The shocks to his gag ring send tears to his eyes and spit up his nose and fill his ears with dog-like choking noises, but he grabs Mike's hips and holds on. His mouth is grappling for the tender strength in their sex, and Mike angles his hips for that same heat, while calling Arrigo filthy, bitter names, snarling, Take it, take it, take it. Because that much is familiar, they both know it, that commandment to endure.

Mike shoves Arrigo off him and stuffs his cock back in his jeans. "You're such a whore," he says, and spits. "Say it, babe. Go ahead and say it."

Dazed, automatically, Arrigo says, "I'm a whore," and cleans his lips with his tongue.

"At first, I couldn't understand it. I thought I knew you. I thought, it can't be he changed his mind."

Mike's dark eyes swim with his failure. Because look, the Vine is dead and no one is any better. Mike has seen his world turn on him again and the only channel in him dug strong enough to carry that much pain is his rage.

"But then, seeing you with Lana and your kid, I get it. You get to play house. The family your parents wanted for you. And what good is that if you can't send them photos and vinecasts of their grandson? You were always chasing them. Because you're a whore, Arrigo—you'll say anything, be anyone, just to get people to make you feel better about yourself."

This is so unjust, so cruel an interpretation of what Arrigo has done for Mike, he has no choice but to confirm it. "Yeah," Arrigo says. "Sure. That's why I did it."

"All that fucking talk about the galactic tide and breaking away from Earth, you were only saying what I wanted to hear."

"You fell for it. Don't you feel like an asshole."

Arrigo pictures his neverhusband as a frail, bitter old man, hunched in his walker, hating him, pissing his pants with hatred. Maybe this is easier, maybe now Arrigo won't have to see it.

Mike spits again. Arrigo leans and spits into the aeration pool. Mike leaves and Arrigo lies on his back. Something enormous gathers in his chest, a thunderhead of heavy, toxic froth. With a crack of inner lightning, the emotion breaks, exiting him in a body spasm that lasts a whole minute, leaving him panting, hollowed out. Notions of exorcism and childbirth are not far from mind as he sprawls, stunned and wondering, until it's time to gather up his dead birds and go.

LANA AND THE ship's veterinarians clone earthworms from subjects in the genetics labs. On greendeck, she bores holes in the soil, feeds in the worms, and covers the holes with stones. In the eucalyptus grove, the feral cats are queening. Lana protects the kittens from their mothers; sometimes cats in distress eat their struggling young, mistaking them for stillborns. She steers the tabby queen's face with her palm, guiding her attention to her healthy litter. "Look, mom. See? This one's alive. This one, and this one here." Lana's chest tightens, holding shattered pieces in place. Crouched along the ferny undergrowth, she smooths the weary mother's fur. "All alive, momma. Look at them go."

In the savannah, the people in the grass stir to eat and drink a little. They sit up, shaking off an enchantment.

EMPTY SPACE IS not empty. At the quantum level, spacetime churns with virtual particles and anti-particles fluctuating into and out of being. Their existence is so small and so fleeting, they are literally unobservable; observation doesn't properly happen in such dimensions. One level up, at the scale of atoms, space is scattered with radiation and matter—cosmic rays and dust, hydrogen ions foamed off stars a hundred trillion miles away. In the long reaches between star systems, this mist of atoms and rays, called the interstellar medium, is usually so diffuse, it's almost not there at all. And this is the key point: that all this presence and busyness in space exists so trivially, so beneath human notice, it's tempting to believe in the nothingness that shows itself to the eye. But mark out sufficient distance and the interstellar medium is heavy as a star; mark out sufficient time and it becomes one. Contrasts in its heat and density form filaments, chimneys, shells. Shapes and winds, even in emptiness. Clouds of matter clump into stars, stars whorl into galaxies, galaxies cluster and supercluster, and superclusters organize into large-scale structures webbing the entire known cosmos—the universe producing structure and change at every scale, out of almost nothing.

We will return to this idea later, at the end.

⁅||||⁆

ACT THREE

They say this opera is too sad, and that there are too many deaths in it.
But after all, everything in life is death! What else is there?
—Letter of Giuseppe Verdi to Countess Maffei, 29 Jan. 1853

Lana is gathering water samples, following a stream in the oak scrub habitat toward the high desert zone, when she stumbles on a wild man with a spear. Definitely not the sort of thing one expects to encounter on a spaceship ten light-years from Earth, but there he is, twenty meters ahead, a shadow against the dusk light. The wild man is Leopold Rosenbaum, erstwhile priest, erstwhile saboteur, presently desert hermit. It's been decades since Lana last saw him. The *Ekphrasis* is more than sixty years into its journey to Qaf, and Leo has spent half of it in a feral, holy privacy. His spear is a slender, sharpened branch. Something flashes as, with a grunt, he stabs it into the streambank. He pumps his fists and sends up a whoop, his bare feet splashing in and out of the water. He goes still, kneels in the middle of the stream, and brings his hands prayerfully together. He stays there a moment, then stands, turns, and beckons to Lana with a hundred-watt smile.

"Hi there! Come see!"

And Lana, mildly embarrassed, makes her way over to see a fat bullfrog speared through the head in the mud.

"Holy shit," Lana says. "Is this what you've been living off of all this time?"

"Not always," Leo demurs. He won't stop smiling.

Sometimes, in the oak forest, Lana finds a basket of bread secured in the crook of a branch. Sometimes she sees Remy collecting empty T injections stashed in the hollows. But Leo is, as far as she can tell, an absolute solitary, a stealthy white hart.

Leo leads her to his cookfire, further into the desert, among the rocks and manzanilla. The coals are smoldering and he alternates between stoking the flames and dressing the bullfrog. She's surprised how much meat he gets off it. Leo notices when her glance flicks disapprovingly over the ribbon of smoke curling into the air.

"Don't worry, I'm careful," he says. "I use fire sparingly, and only when it's time."

Lana frowns. "Who tells you when it's time for a fire?"

"The grass, usually," he says, not looking up.

The desert cools as their longitude rotates into night. Lana refastens her paisley wrap around her shoulders, over her corduroy jacket; middle age has coaxed her into a soft butch. "And the bullfrogs? What do they tell you?"

Leo transfers the frog meat into a cookpot, considering. "How to catch them. When they need catching—you know, Lana, they've been encroaching on other habitats for years. They shouldn't be this far into the oak scrub or they'll push out the others. It's lucky for you I've been here to check them." He finally looks up, his smile tentative. "You think I'm crazy?"

"No. Well, a little."

She is thinking of how the communities on greendeck speak to her, in their soft ways. Halfway to Qaf, twenty years ago, she'd realized the biome modeling was so twisted up, it had to be scrapped and rebuilt. The models were designed with Earth data, which had seemed reasonable at the time. But there are biogeochemical cycles completing a thousand times faster here than on Earth. There are other, wholly artificial cycles with their own Frankenstein gaits. After decades of watching the simulations run off the rails and scrambling to correct, Lana saw greendeck had gone its own way. Her teams reconstructed the models from first principles, with data gathered only from the *Ekphrasis*. The grass tells you when it needs burning: it wasn't that different from the spooky crap Leo was describing, in the end. "It's like raising a child, isn't it?"

"I suppose." Leo sits back and cuts up a wild onion. "I'll admit, I've had some harsh words for the bullfrog. Things I needed to say at the time. But it's a wonderful creature. God's slimy, big-bellied children. It saved my life. I really almost starved."

"You didn't almost starve, Leo. You could have gone downstairs any time and had rice and beans with the rest of us."

"I couldn't." He shakes his head firmly. "You know that's not true."

"Some people thought you'd died."

And Leo gives her a serious look, as if to say, Maybe I did. This, finally, is too much for her.

"Oh, I get it, right—you're born again? In Christ?" His face falls, which provokes Lana all the more. "In Space Jesus?"

Leo braces his hands on his knees and watches her, not responding, not particularly serene, but waiting for her to understand that her rudeness—her lack of curiosity—has disinvited her. Fair enough. It's an old story; Lana accepts it more or less graciously. She stands, brushing the sand from her ass. Sorry, she says, and Leo nods. From inside the blue desert dusk, Lana has a clear view up the side of greendeck that's still in sun. At the grassland's transition, a familiar figure crouches and sits at the wailing line.

"Is that Arrigo?" Lana says. She recognizes the hair.

"Yes. He comes out here often. He's taught me a great deal, too."

"He visits you? You talk to him?"

"No," says the hermit. "Not yet. But soon."

ONLY DAYS UNTIL the ground dips from under Arrigo's feet. In a few light-dark cycles, the ship's fore engines will initiate a twenty-year deceleration, and the floors will tilt into a new one-percent grade declining toward Qaf. All the subtle postures the crew forgot in forty-two years of level floors will have to be relearned in reverse. Old trees will grow like parentheses and the planet ahead will be a bottom tugging at their steps, less a heaven than a settling, a roll coming to a stop. Death, not to put too fine a point on it. This is what we signed up for, Arrigo thinks, to die dazzled under an alien sun.

Qaf fills everyone's imagination. Hall Q's holographic model is projected in miniature across homedeck: a fixture in galleries, a centerpiece on dining tables. In one abstract series, mounted outside the astrochemistry labs, the planet manifests as a giant mandala crowding black brushstrokes into the panels' corners. In a mural allegory, its red sun is an immense rose held by a woman with no breasts. Painters pester the astronomers for more details. Luyten's Star is dimmer than our Sun, the system's habitable zone hugs its host star unnervingly close, so Qaf's sun in the sky should look ten times as large as Earth's. Its oceans should iridesce a gentle, purple blush, not the harsh white spatter of Earth-waters.

As for Arrigo, Qaf flickers into his poems as a wing, a snow, a stone.

He steals into a lonely part of greendeck, notebook in hand. He sits, and he pictures his heart as a Christmas tree weighed down with ornaments. The snowman is his loneliness, the angels anger, the sleighs and sacks are cumbered with grief, the shining ruby balls gleam hopelessness. One by one, he unhooks the emotion and gets it out of him, trembling, clenching, rolling, yawning. It's alarmingly physical work, his own private mad scene. When it's done, the boughs of his heart are bare and he listens for the poem to sing itself into being.

In homedeck's concert auditorium, the Qaf hologram, rotating and updating, suspends over the dark piles of seats and balconies like a chandelier. Every year, the image feels closer: as if Arrigo could take a running jump and touch it. He fastens the snaps of Elkeid's corset and asks him, "Do you ever dream of flying?"

On the stage, around them, chorus singers mill and mark in half-costume, wearing topcoats and crinolines over t-shirts and colorful cloth streamers where monkey brush and passion-flower vines will hang. Arrigo is producing a revised *La Traviata in the Amazon* for its 50th anniversary. With his help, Melsinger has rewritten a majority of Act II and several crucial passages in Acts I and III, including the final chorus of shades. The rehearsing dead sing under their breath, toneless, eyes wandering, as if searching out a pitch in the fly loft.

Elkeid says, "I dream of digging."

The revision is exacting, unpredictable work. Maestro Melsinger's aesthetic has evolved over six decades in space; also, he is dying. Neither man acknowledges this silent partner, but his cancer forces

Melsinger (ever scrupulous, ever allergic to false notes) to reprosecute the notions of art and mortality he wrote into the original opera at the tender age of fifty-seven. Life, as usual, takes too much: Arrigo has lost M.E., is losing Melsinger, and must assume his parents are long dead, on the other end of a long-dead Vine. These losses cut divots out of him—except, M.E. would say that the opposite is true, that in a rigorous and unsentimental way, Arrigo carries forward M.E.'s being as an ineluctable addition to him, because of how their life has informed his. This is, after all, how he knows what M.E. would say. Melsinger, too, has a virtual life inside Arrigo; the words for his frontier opera, once so hopelessly out of reach, run like a brook in Arrigo's imagination, softly, inevitably vital.

Elkeid will sing the lead soprano role. His voice never dropped—another quirk of the in utero vitacene—and with Arrigo's help, he has trained it into something new and superb. Like a Falcon soprano, with the eerie, marbled quality of a castrato. Life, as always, gives more than Arrigo deserves: Elkeid is more than a son, far stranger and better, merging man and woman, child and adult, protégé and peer, brother-in-arms and Queen of the Night. Due to Elkeid's partial dosing, he and Arrigo present as the same age now, handsomely forty-six. Elkeid's features hold a mirror to Arrigo's own, maling and unmaling his face in turn.

Arrigo had never meant to be much of a father. The profile he cultivated was more "eccentric uncle": he'd swan in and play old opera recordings, eager to hear what grotesque novelties the boy discovered in them. Then Elkeid hit his confounding puberty and Arrigo was unexpectedly, perversely useful, his endless, mazy notioning over queerness, divergent natures, and revised constructs suddenly urgent to this star-child he loved. What would it mean, he'd asked when Elkeid was a baby, for him to grow up with gravity directed outward into the stars, not down to a planetary core? To form his personhood flung away from center, no Earth under his feet, but the expanse of the universe—how would it affect his mind, or not his mind, but his identity, his being? (His *soul*, Arrigo.)

They went together to see Leo on his pillar. After leaving the brig, but before retreating into greendeck's wilderness, for ten years Leo lived on a small platform at the top of a pillar he made from a dead birch tree and scrap metal, erected where the savannah transitions into desert. Younger star-children liked to come and stick flowers, branches, and feathers into this pillar, turning it ornate, fractal-structured, with little pillars branching off and even smaller pillars sticking out of their sides, and on each, a tiny effigy of the Leo the Stylite: a green plastic soldier, a crabapple pome, a violet, two sticks tied together with thread. Leo would scowl down and swing a long stick at them, and they'd hop back and jaw like crows in their secret language. But when Arrigo took Elkeid there, they were the only visitors. The hermit was standing, his arms outstretched, his palms to the sunline, and his eyes hooded.

Leo never spoke, except the thanks he gave whenever taking up the bread and water his friends lifted in a basket on a pole (or passing down the bucket his friends gingerly received). It's the kind of thing that sounds deranged, but once you witness it, it bowls you over. Lana cried.

Arrigo had a whole speech prepared for Elkeid, the moral being that the ship will support such extremes that whatever wild new thing he is, he will be embraced and cared for. In the shadow of Leo's pillar, though, in the hot, starchy grass, they sat and didn't speak at all. They plucked and wound dry blades around their fingers and absorbed the silence Leo had worked so hard to nourish. Within that silence, Arrigo sensed the presence of another lesson in the grass with them, one he wasn't yet equipped to understand.

He'd looked up at the pillar-hermit. Maybe this stylus was Leo's penance, to model the lost ship's peculiar, public solitude. The height was seclusion, but also notoriety. Years later, Leo must have decided his penance was miscarrying—when they started calling him Saint Leo—and he fled into the desert.

The *Ekphrasis* still sends signals down the Vine, never answered. Calling, singing into the dark.

La Traviata in Space

So, what about large-scale structure? Violetta and Alfredo fall in love, they break up, they reconcile, she dies—why does that feel like an opera instead of warmed-over gossip? I want to tease out one aspect of that story-shape, which is important to *La Traviata in the Amazon* and Melsinger's rewrite, and it has to do with the harmonics of Violetta's death.

That finale is in D-flat major, a key Verdi uses in only a few other, significant places: it's the key in which Germont, the voice of social convention, sings his stodgy, come-home-son aria, "Di Provenza il mar," and tells Violetta, *Give up this seductive dream.* Meanwhile, a lot of the opera's most enchanting music—including Violetta's "Sempre libera"—is in A-flat major. Now, D-flat and A-flat are a perfect fifth apart, an interval so fundamental to Western music, I can't even begin to capture how rich this connection is. But if you've heard any classical music, you've heard that *thing* at the end of a piece, where the music flies up into a sort of suspension (*bum!*), then falls back down with a satisfying crash (*bwaaah!!*), and then everyone knows the symphony is over. That's a closed cadence, a musical punctuation mark. The final chord (the *bwaaah!!*) is the "tonic" chord, built on the tonic, or first pitch, of the key. The chord before it, the one that sounds like someone tossed a ball in the air, is the "dominant" chord, built on the dominant pitch of that key. What's the dominant pitch? Well, it's the pitch a perfect fifth above the tonic. So, say you're Beethoven, finishing a movement in D-flat major, your final progression will be an A-flat chord, creating a sense of suspension, expectation, dissonance, that resolves in a D-flat chord, with its corresponding sense of release and completion.

That's what Verdi does in the finale of *La Traviata*. The doctor, the maid, Alfredo, and an apologetic Germont are gathered around Violetta's couch as she swoons through her last breaths; the ensemble's music is in D-flat, the "Di Provenza" key. Suddenly, Violetta revives— she's full of life again!—the strings rise chromatically, and the orchestra churns out A-flat chords like crazy (remember, the "Sempre libera" key), and Violetta holds a high A-flat . . .! Then it all comes crashing down: Violetta dies, and the dominant A-flat chord resolves into D-flat chords—they're D-flat minor, though, a tragic modulation of the tonic—which the orchestra smashes into our ears as the curtain falls. The end: Violetta's wayward life is a fleeting, unstable dissonance that can only collapse into the tragic force of conformity.

For the original *La Traviata in the Amazon*, Melsinger plays off this ending while offering a different thesis. The final scene is the Italian troupe's soprano performing "Sempre libera" for the Manaus élite in the Teatro Amazonas, surrounded by a chorus of the dead: her fellow singers, her lover Maria, the rubber tappers. The chorus of shades sings nonsense words, incoherence, the language of the dead, in pitches that add up to musical chaos—there's no key, no tonal center—while her voice hurtles over them, the artist struggling against the universe's entropy to carve out some moment of beauty. We all liked it. It felt like a solid, queer response to Verdi's bleak closed cadence. The music never resolves into Germont's key, but stays centered, if anywhere, in Violetta's A-flat major. Violetta, or at least the artist inhabiting her, is not required to die; she persists in the face of a death-driven universe.

For the revised *La Traviata in the Amazon*, though, I feel like I'm missing something. There is still the same scenario, Violetta and "Sempre libera" and the chorus of shades, but it sounds different, as if the soprano's key modulates out of A-flat, although her melody line looks the same as before. Melsinger is no help, the smug old coot, watching me strain to hear it with a merry glint in his eyes and a smile forming in his loose, cloudy beard.

ARRIGO WALKS BY himself through the thoroughly greened halls of homedeck. Whole corridors have become dirt paths under hanging arbors and vines; rain spills in, blown by steady winds. In the night hours, it smells like jasmine. A chalky aroma of dirt kicked up under his shoes, dew on fat mushrooms blistering out of decayed hotel furniture. Arrigo sees blooms he's sure he's never known on Earth. Strong-smelling lilacs as big as beehives and giant peonies like yolks of color. Spectacles of vitality, a gaudy thriving signaling to others the stores of life in their folds.

In one of homedeck's corridors (he doesn't know which), people have seen a giant lady in a black mantle kneeling around a spilling basket of flowers. Arrigo doesn't see her tonight, but there is someone at his door, waiting.

An old man, stout but well-postured, in a short-sleeve linen button-down. His potbelly strains at the placket and his arms, thin and brown, are scrawled in the weathered green-black of old tattoos. His hair is a bright silver, but his lashes are as long and dark as a girl's.

"Mike?"

Mike holds Arrigo's gaze, defensive. He is ready to bolt if Arrigo looks away, which is all Arrigo wants to do.

It's been forty-two years since he and Mike split; thirty-five years since the last word they spoke, something like "Excuse me" when they bumped into each other in the kitchens. It's hard avoiding someone on a ship of only twenty-four hundred people. But they've done it. Mike's made a social burrow out of his fellow engineers, a rowdy, sharp crowd. Whenever Arrigo's spotted Mike, at a gallery show or a dance, he turns young and wretched; his self-possession melts, his bones vanish, and he flops into a puddle of need. So, he's kept his distance. He has no intention of turning back into the person who'd do anything for Mike to forgive him.

"You look good," Arrigo says, which of course is the worst thing to say. It's true, Mike looks amazing, considering—but it's that considering that is so terrible. Mike, in his eighties (?), is "debonair," "active," "spry": words used only to describe people who have lived past their time. Mike endures Arrigo's admiration. His gaze skips across Arrigo's ageless body and that old, furious pride roils into his expression. Arrigo unlocks the door and gets Mike inside before he can change his mind.

"You go first," Mike says. "I move slower these days."

"Take your time," Arrigo says, and Mike does, as if the floor will lurch out from under his feet. Which it will, but not for twelve more hours at least.

"I wasn't waiting for long." Mike enunciates in a careful, wondering voice, like he can't believe it himself. "I stopped by, hoping to find you at home. And then, there you were, coming around the corner."

He raises his voice too loud; he is probably going deaf. And he takes forever to get through a sentence, with a whole facial dance of brow-knitting and blinks. He is himself, but a codger. His personality has taken on a certain stoniness and sunk to the bottom of something.

"Your place is clean," Mike says, not hiding his surprise.

Arrigo's apartment is tidy, colorful and enthusiastically decorated, but, he's proud to show Mike, he hasn't reverted to the cluttered, manic living space of his twenties. They find one of the smaller star-children in a cupboard and chase him out. Star-children born these later years are always in strange places—in hatches, up trees, under your bed.

He makes tea from a jar of dried nettle. "I'm really trying to get into tea," Arrigo says.

Mike says something, but too quietly. He clears his throat, winces, tries again.

"Lana told me why, told me about . . ." His words fail.

Arrigo's stomach drops. This is it: they are doing this. What should have happened decades ago, it's happening now. Arrigo isn't prepared, he is holding a pink ceramic tea-mug like an asshole. Mike scowls, indicating himself up and down: "Why you wanted the Vine intact. I was unfair to you."

Arrigo sets the mug down and straightens. "When did she tell you?"

Mike grimaces. "About six years ago. Look—it didn't exactly make me eager to see you, right? Knowing you were so horrified by me aging naturally, you'd blow up our relationship and turn in our friends to stop it. Didn't exactly inspire me the way she expected it to."

"Oh, Mike," Arrigo says, embracing him, pressing his face in the crook of Mike's neck. "Leo was more your friend," he says. "I mean, I respect him, but I don't believe in God—you know—"

"Obviously. Can we sit down?"

Arrigo retrieves an extra cushion from off his bed.

"You were still wrong to do what you did," Mike calls from the living room. "I'm not going to apologize for being mad at you. What, you think I didn't notice the vitacene dosing was off? I knew before I met you. I mean, why do you think *I* was in sick bay that day? Remy and I have been working on this for ages." Arrigo reenters with the cushion, trembling. Mike is testing his wrist, working the joint back and forth. "You couldn't just talk to me and respect my ability to deal with my own vitacene-rejecting body. No, you had to go off and do some grand operatic tragic-romance bullshit, it's exactly the sort of false consciousness we wanted to quarantine on Earth." Mike lifts, slides the cushion on to the chair, and sits again, blinking. "What, am I talking too much?"

Arrigo sits next to Mike and holds both his hands. "I'm sorry. It's—I'm so happy to see you again. I don't care how mad you are, that's fine, I'm just glad you're talking to me."

His face, the face Arrigo knows with his eyes closed, is crumpled with wrinkles and sags in unkind places. He has deep grooves and planes under his eyes, as if a kid with a pocketknife had carved him out of wood—as if time, which has so finely worked on the rest of them, used Mike as its practice scrap.

"I was brutal to you," he says. "I should—look, I'm sorry about it."

"Water under the bridge."

"It's not," Mike says, "but you can say it is, for now. It felt like the time to take care of unfinished business." His gaze drifts sidelong. "Before the Big Dip, I mean. Don't you think?"

He says this as if he's making rounds, as if some next piece of business is waiting for him. Arrigo says, "You're not going, are you?"

It's not like Arrigo's been holding out four decades for him. Pining, madame-butterflying, rehearsing their fourteen-minute reconciliation duet: no. He's had boyfriends and crushes, the usual. But the lack of resolution between him and Mike has always disappointed him, the preposterous holes they'd left in each other's stories.

Mike asks, "How long do you want me to stay?"

The worry darts shyly from Mike's eyes. His vulnerability shocks Arrigo. What it must cost him. Arrigo doesn't know how to answer. Or, rather, he knows how to reassure Mike, how to please him or say what he thinks will please him. He pictures what it would be to kiss his old unhusband now, or to get down on the floor and suck at his gnarled cock, or to fuck, gently and carefully, to lay pillows under tricky joints. He figures any desire or kindness he withholds from Mike's elderly body will be a curse he lays on his own old age. And to be honest, he's not uncurious. But he's also not ready to do any of that, and he's not being asked to, either. Mike is asking him about time.

"Longer," Arrigo says, and his throat tightens. Tears pearl under his eyes.

MIKE ENDS UP staying the night. By the time their conversation flags, he's so tired, Arrigo insists he sleep in the bed, while Arrigo takes the couch. They talk about Qaf, of course. Despite the inhibited dosing, Mike's vitacene worked a little. Remy estimates that Mike is in his early seventies physiologically, so there's some chance he could live to see planetfall. Arrigo talks about real sunlight on their faces and the smell of ocean fog, and Mike reminds him the sun will be dimmer, and there's no guarantee the air will be breathable.

But you'll see it with us, Arrigo asks him, in masks or suits or whatever, and yes—Mike hesitates, but Arrigo's smile draws the word from him, *yes*—if everything works out, Mike'll be down there with the rest of them.

Bedding down alone, curled over old couch cushions, Arrigo lets the dismay and grief he's been holding back pour out. It's not all for Mike. The mortal condition wallops Arrigo like some terrible surprise each time. Arrigo stayed with M.E. through the very end of their cancer, and now he's seeing Melsinger down the same difficult path. At the time, he'd thought M.E., as a philosopher, would be prepared to meet death with a rational system, but no, the pain and ugliness of the body giving out unraveled them. *Please*, they begged, their chewed nails digging into his wrist, eyes popping, red and baby-blue. *Please*, I don't want to, I'm so afraid. Now, to see Mike wearing his own mortality so nakedly—Donne was mistaken: death is awfully proud. Arrigo cries silently, careful not to be heard. Why does every opera end with a heap of bodies on the stage? Well, not really. There are the comic operas. But mortality haunts the form. Maybe, rather, it acts as a counterweight, balancing the music's explosive life against death's gravity. Or maybe that same gravity, death's sureness and solidity gives the music its grandeur and purpose, serves as a rigid structure for us to ornament. Death structures our life and beauty dresses it.

I am undonne, he thinks, drifting into unconsciousness.

As for Mike, the smell of Arrigo's sleep on the sheets instantly relaxes him, and he drops into a dreamless space.

HERE IS WHAT Mike's been up to in the last forty-odd years: he worked on the ship, mostly. He kept to himself and aged. Even after the Vine investigation cleared him, he was notorious, so he tended to rebuff shows of sympathy or sexual interest as lurid. He brought food for Leo on his pillar, but Leo didn't talk to him. He went to prayer meetings with other priestless Catholics and listened to the other Filipinos describe Holy Week processions in Manila and Naga. In Bicol, they told him, where his grandmother lived, there is a holy effigy of Christ-in-death that heals the sick. A childless woman of great piety raised it from a shapeless piece of wood, like a son, and by a miracle, it grew into Christ's form taken down from the Cross and it even walked the region for a time, but now is too old. He made friends with Carolyn Red Deer, over beers and a shared distaste for the Lana-and-Arrigo show. It was Carolyn who got him working on the long-range spectroscopes and the Hoopoe probe, a Vine transponder refitted as a space probe they could send ahead to Qaf. He drew a comic book called *Nighttown* about an oppressed underclass living on the outside of a Dyson sphere. He learned Tagalog after all, and for real, and even Bikol too. He exercised. He stayed limber. He was in the room with Carolyn when their world began to fall apart, one final time.

In the morning, Mike is seated opposite the couch when Arrigo stirs. "I need to tell you something about Qaf," Mike says, quickly and smoothly, like he's practiced.

Arrigo turns and looks for the hologram floating in the middle of his table.

It is unrecognizable, red and yellow and gray like a bruise.

CAROLYN RED DEER races bad news up the ship, finding her friends and exes before the rumors hit them unprepared. It's one reading, she tells Lana. It's an outlier. The model assigns greater weight to the most recent telemetry, so the Hall Q simulation is getting ahead of itself. Carolyn makes encouraging faces like she's trying them in a mirror. Her jet-black brows nearly fly away, she arches them so high. The chances of Qaf actually being like what the last spectroscopic reading shows, while producing every previous reading in error— she can't even begin to calculate it. It's low, astronomically low.

So, what does the last spectroscopic reading show, Carolyn? "Methane and carbon dioxide atmosphere. Sulfuric acid clouds. Massive, relentless volcanic activity. Surface temperatures over 400 centigrade. We can't see how it could support water, much less complex life. It's *angry*."

Lana shuts off her hearing aids and closes her eyes. Silence rings and whines.

"You said it's an outlier," Lana says, as she switches her aids on again. "What are the chances of the planet being like what we thought it was, and producing *this* reading in error?"

Carolyn slumps. "Astronomically low."

Alone, hurrying, Lana considers her next steps. Most of what she'd do in this situation is already underway. They've been anticipating a MSME around the transition to deceleration; the food stores are full, oxygen levels slightly high, pods assigned, and crew are already gathering on greendeck. But there's more to do. *She* needs to do more. Losing Qaf—it's worse than losing Earth. The thought worms into her inner body, leaving an airy borehole in its wake, a tunnel of faintness and cold needling through her. The miracle of Qaf's alien life spun from original forms—a pile of volcanic ash. A raging hellscape.

(Earth is not necessarily lost, by the way—but Lana treats Earth as lost to her, whatever its true situation. This is the only sane meaning of distance.)

Lana stoops and catches her breath against an old wardrobe overgrown in clematis. I can bear it, she tells the wardrobe. She smacks it with the heel of her palm. The rotten structure rattles, then groans with a human voice.

Inside the wardrobe, Arrigo is curled into a corner, his chest pumping with rapid breaths.

"Jesus, already?" Lana says.

Down the hall, Mike Faustino turns a corner. They see each other and Mike holds up his hands: I come in peace.

"Is he in there?" Mike calls. "I couldn't keep up with him."

"I needed to get away," Arrigo says, panting.

Here is what Arrigo knows: that his work for the last sixty years has been to unwrap from the structures he clings to for support, or they will be wrenched out from under him. What he has failed to learn in time is that his vision of Qaf as a misfit paradise was one more trellis he's held on to for too long. Now he is left a disaster; now his life is a lonely, ridiculous thing; now he knows the only way this farce could have ended is in a heap of bodies on the stage.

Crying suits Arrigo. He has the face for it, with his high watershed nose and weeping-willow curls. His eyes are red-rimmed and his voice has dropped an octave. "I'm missing memories of Earth," he says, the words breaking across sobs. "Can't remember my old house, my room, what pictures were along the stairs. I can't remember Boston at all. I have, like, this sticky sense on my skin of summer air along the Charles . . ." Lana has never met any man less interested in holding back tears; it's a superpower. Arrigo's crying and rambling overtake each other, he rushes through the one to make room for the other. "And that's it. Bodies of water. Miles and miles of it. The way they blinded you in the sun with diamonds—" His eyes squeeze shut and overflow.

Mike and Lana help him to his feet. Arrigo runs his fingertips under the wardrobe's hanging flowers.

"You should come with us to greendeck," he says to Lana, hiccoughing.

"Later, maybe. I've got to talk to the committees about moving up rapid-response measures, then organize the biome walk-through, then check the auxiliary systems . . ."

"No, no, you need to come to greendeck." Arrigo turns to Mike. "She's doing that thing where she acts as if she's responsible for everything and makes herself busy so she doesn't have a quiet moment to feel as terrible as she does." Arrigo is still crying, but he has a wild, unaimed perceptivity he swings around him. "This clematis needs pruning."

Lana softens. "I'll go," she says.

The crew now knows to gather on greendeck during a MSME. There is a chosen spot, under St. Leo's abandoned pillar, where people congregate. Where they can feel hard earth under them and listen to the wind in the tall grass. *La ligne des larmes*, it's called. The wailing line. It's night when the three of them arrive. The sunline is shielded, but the day-side's albedo is bright as a moon, making the packed sand between the chaparral glow white. People make their way from across the ship, tall shadows parting the grass. They drop and breathe in its hay-like musk. The nones pass between them with tea thermoses and linen bags of crackers. Their robes whisk over the stalks. Crickets sing, not far away. A none's shaved head gleams as she bends to a hand lifting out of the grass.

The Vine's severance didn't stop these episodes, but it forced everyone to confront the phenomenon more nakedly. No better teacher than silence. There's a super-structure to them, just as M.E. suspected: coherence obscurely ordered, hard to explain, but it's there. Like the enigmatic large-scale cosmic structures that span the universe, galactic clusters and superclusters separated by billions of light years forming even larger cosmic filaments and knots, into an unthinkably giant web, structure at the scale of the whole observable universe. There is nothing sane about such distances. These structures speak to interconnectedness not as a sentimentality, not as a virtue to practice or fail to practice, but as a matter of nature, of inevitability. Shapefulness and mutual influence are cosmic law, change and churn spoil apartness, and things cannot help but fall into being. Just so, there is a coherence between every living particular being on the *Ekphrasis*, human, bird, mangrove, worm, spanning the mutual incomprehensibility of other minds, nothing magical, but a subtle rhythm of networks, a scheme of faint harmonies, the way yawns are contagious, in the same way so is grief, so is courage, so is the vital force.

Arrigo cries in a ball in the grass until he's shivering. Lana runs her hand along his back. Shadows of feral cats dart across the desert scape like shooting stars.

"So, how are you doing? Honestly," Mike says to her.

"About Qaf?"

"This has to be, what, your worst nightmare? You OK?"

"It's a challenge," Lana says. She sits cross-legged in the grass and squints up at an acacia forest suspended on day-side. A breeze rolls through its bright treetops and the grass around her ripples as if in echo. "Not my worst nightmare. Not for a long time. This dumb bottled biome and I have been through so many nightmares together. You OK?"

Mike gestures up and down his own uncooperative body. "I think I relate. Yeah."

(Do you want to know Mike's worst nightmare? It has always been this: that Qaf would turn out to be the same Earth he'd left. Call it parallel planetary evolution, call it determinism, that's the thought that terrifies him. A perfect double of Earth, another Earth-like civilization. Another New Eden, Arizona waiting for him. With white, tidy houses on well-paved streets lined with maples, and front gardens shining with every bloom and sweet herb, waiting.)

Old man Mike lowers himself gingerly into the grass. He coughs and cackles as his seat drops the last inch.

"Guess no walks on the beach—" Arrigo tries to joke, but his voice fails.

"Hey." Mike leans and takes Arrigo's hands in his. "Who are we? We're faggots. The world doesn't have to be good for us to be all right."

Mike's hands are cold and tough like a branch. The knuckles are knobby and the frame of fingerbones palpable through the skin. Time is a wind and Mike has grown resilient in it.

Beyond their little circle, St. Leo himself comes forth out of the desert to join the nones' work along the wailing line. Mike exclaims wordlessly, and Arrigo feels his tired skin rouse into goosepimples. No loincloths, no camelskins; his beard is light and thin; but Leo moves through the grass with the feverish grace of a glorified soul, a beauty weathered and dense with credible gospel. Watching him, Arrigo understands why he brought Elkeid to see Leo on his pillar so many years ago. The lesson wasn't about acceptance, but magnificence.

Arrigo and Lana catch each other having the same idea.

"What?"

"You go first," Arrigo says.

"I was thinking," Lana says, "it'll be years before we know for sure—but even if Qaf is as barren and hellish as the new telemetry says, I want to see it. See its acid clouds, its volcanos, all of it."

Arrigo nods emphatically. "It's going to be astonishing."

"And if we can fall into a stable orbit, we'll still have fuel to power the sunline for decades more. Maybe photovoltaics or harvested atmosphere could power it even farther. We could maintain the biome indefinitely."

Leo, breaking from his rounds, joins the three of them and they make a compass in the grass. Arrigo picks a bug off Mike's shoulder and sets it in the dust. Leo is musky and ripe, his white shirt stained with dirt and green matter and his bare feet browned and thick with calluses like hooves. Mike is shy around him, but Lana asks, with more than a little bluster, Well, did you find God? and Leo says, Oh, yes. Then he decides to play along: Funny, it's always the last place you look, isn't it? Leo has thrived in the wilderness. There's starlight in his eyes. He's showing us it can be done, Arrigo thinks. We'll circle the scorched planet, apart but connected, anchored in Qaf's gravity but riding our own velocity, not belonging to any paradise but the one we've created on the ship.

Mike, too, studies Leo. He takes a deep breath and faces each of them in turn. "Harvesting atmosphere," he says. "Lana's right—it could power the sunline. It could power a signal, too."

Some time back, he explains, he and Carolyn Red Deer, experimenting with optical data transmission systems for the Hoopoe probe, realized that if they pointed a laser of sufficient power at Earth, they could re-establish a data link—in that direction, at least—sending messages by rapidly flicking it on and off, like old electrical telegraphy, or signal fires.

Arrigo stares. For Mike to even theorize about reconnecting to Earth suggests an interior shift that would have been impossible when he knew him. It's bittersweet, that this reconciliation happened away from Arrigo, likely by necessity; one more price for his lack of trust. But, here they are now. They haven't let each other's hands go. Something golden shuttles between them through their palms' contact, palms' heat, their solid longtime grip.

The problem was fuel, Mike says, and attention. Most interstellar optical signal designs relied on series of nanosecond bursts so that the laser wouldn't require an outrageous amount of energy, but that assumed a receiver watching for an extremely brief, faint signal, with extremely sensitive telescopes. Catching the attention of people on Earth who weren't expecting anything would take more energy than the ship had to spare. But with an unlimited supply of combustible gas—that could work.

"What would that look like?" Lana asks. "On Earth?"

"Any observatory looking at Canis Minor would catch it. It helps that Luyten's Star is so dim. Then they'd notice a pattern—we'd put a pattern in it, and say: Here we are."

"We're here, we're queer, get used to it," Arrigo says, smiling.

"Oh my God, shut up," Lana says. "Mike—what if there aren't functioning observatories? What if something terrible did happen, and humans on Earth are back to living as nomads and subsistence farmers?"

Mike considers. "Then we'll be a new star, with a flickering light."

Leo breaks into an innocent grin. "A new star of Bethlehem!" he exclaims, and everyone groans, but Arrigo's pleased, because after forty years in the desert, Leo is still the guy who takes things too far.

A long time ago, Leo asked him how queerness propagates, and this is Arrigo's answer: aesthetically. Our thriving produces beauty and that beauty signals to others that there is life in this way of being. That's how we persist across generations, by inspiring others like us into self-honesty. So, it's important to show Earth that we're alive: look, it can be done, we got here, we are thriving, we love you, hello. Whatever struggles you're facing on Earth, look up. Behold. A beacon, a star to catch the eye and set the mind to wondering. A scented handkerchief, "*designedly dropt*,"

Bearing the owner's name someway in the corners, that one may see and remark, and say Whose?

In the distance, a figure scales Leo's pillar in a ballgown. The desert night turns its wearer into a giant bird ascending. When Elkeid reaches the joggy platform, he balances and stands upright, and sings the Act III finale from Melsinger's opera, not Violetta's part but the chorus of shades' odd, atomic scribbles of melody. Without the soprano's through-line, these pieces sound more like birdsong than composition, and the grief-stricken in the grass pause and crane and listen with the consolation of expecting nothing, understanding nothing. Except now Arrigo hears it—what Melsinger wants him to hear—faint triads emerge out of the scattered elements, nothing declarative, but a gentle web of coherences in—F major, he thinks, the key of the "Di quell'amor" theme, *that love which is the heartbeat of the entire universe* . . . As Elkeid sings, Arrigo—and Lana and Mike, and Leopold, and all the expedition gathered—are witnessing some new song form out of the desert.

Slowly but firmly, the ground tips under them, pointing them down, forward, into their new world.

ACKNOWLEDGMENTS

I am grateful to my editor, Deborah Ghim, for her wise and rigorous shepherding of this book into its best form, and to my agent, Kirby Kim, whose faith in this book and tireless advocacy made it happen. Thank you to Signe Swanson, Alexis Nowicki, and the entire Astra House team for your stellar work, and to Rodrigo Corral, for the cover that thrilled me at first sight.

These stories owe a great deal to their original editors, C.C. Finlay, John Joseph Adams, Wendy Wagner, and Carmen Maria Machado, and to my cohorts in the Clarion workshop in San Diego and the Lighthouse Writers Workshop in Denver. Thank you especially to Ren Arcamone, Amanda Baldenaux, Patrick Doerksen, Amy Parker, C.S. Peterson, and Sanjena Sathian for reading (far too many) drafts of these stories over the years, and for your friendship. Additional thanks to Rae Carson, Cory Doctorow, Nalo Hopkinson, Jenny Offill, and Shelley Streeby for your guidance on these stories.

For their generosity in answering my increasingly absurd technical and factual questions, thank you to Matthew Aucoin, Jaime Hernandez, Anju Manandhar, Kirstie Bellman, Patrick McCombs, and Chris Landauer. I am indebted to the research of Peter Wilson, Annulla Linders, and Julian Go on early twentieth-century policing and capital punishment; Timothy Teyler and Jerry Rudy on memory indexing; and, of course, Jack Halberstam's incomparable queer scholarship. Sarah Pinsker's superb generation-ship story, "Wind Will Rove," was an invaluable touchstone for my own thinking.

My path to writing fiction was a circuitous one, and I never would have made it here without the love of literature, technical craft, and audacity that I learned from formative teachers and friends, especially Kathryn Shevelow, Sharon O'Callaghan, William Haywood Henderson, Emily Sinclair, Alexander Lumans, and Robin Black. Thank you to Andrea Dupree and Mike Henry for fostering the community at Lighthouse that got me to take writing seriously, and to the Clarion Foundation for keeping its workshop vibrant and accessible to wide-eyed miscreants all over.

Finally, there are the people whose wisdom, influence, and encouragement helped me bring these stories to their present life: Mom, Dad, and Chris, Michael Kalikow, George Hodgman, and Doug Grand, thank you. And thank you to my love, friend, and partner Rony Lenis, whose fearlessness and artistry gave me the courage to pick up my pencil, and whose support, faith, and patience made this book possible at all.

PHOTO BY CARLY TOPAZIO

ABOUT THE AUTHOR

Theodore McCombs's stories have appeared in *Guernica*, *The Magazine of Fantasy and Science Fiction*, and the anthology *Best American Science Fiction and Fantasy*. Born in Thousand Oaks, California, he is a graduate of the University of California, San Diego, the University of California, Berkeley School of Law, and the Clarion Science Fiction & Fantasy Writers Workshop. He lives in San Diego with his partner and their surly old cat.